A Long Year of Silence

A Long Year of Silence

Kathryn Adams Doty

Edinborough Press

Edinborough Press

1-888-251-6336

www. edinborough. com

books@edinborough. com

LIBRARY OF CONGRESS CATALOGING-IN-PUBLICATION DATA

Doty, Kathryn Adams, 1920-

A long year of silence / Kathryn Adams Doty.— 1st ed.

p. cm.

ISBN 1-889020-13-3 (pbk. : alk. paper)

1. Germany—Foreign public opinion, American—Fiction. 2. World War, 1914-1918—Minnesota—Fiction. 3. Children of clergy—Fiction. 4. German Americans—Fiction. 5. New Ulm (Minn.)—Fiction. 6. Teenage girls—Fiction. I. Title.

PS3604.O89L66 2004

813'.54—dc22

2004004290

An Historic Note by Daniel J. Hoisington.

The text is composed in Adobe Warnock and printed on acid free paper.

Cover:

Girl in a Blue Dress

Henrietta Barclay Paist (ca. 1920)

Used with permission of the Minnesota Historical Society.

Contents

Acknowledgments

THIS HISTORICAL FICTION was inspired by my mother and father, the Anna and Christian of this book. Their love, courage and wisdom lives in every page and I am deeply grateful to them.

I am appreciative, too, to Linda Strauss of the Institute of Children's Literature for launching me on the journey.

The stories my mother told have been verified by the research I have done with the warm and generous assistance of Darla Gebhardt of the Brown County Historical Society, LaVern J. Rippley of Saint Olaf College, Northfield, Minnesota, and Don Heinrich Tolzmann from the University of Cincinnati.

Special thanks to Dr. Ted Fritsche and his wife, Lois, for the gracious use of their time for interviews about the sad and turbulent years in New Ulm during WWI. Since Dr. Fritsche's death on December 5, 2003, I realize more than ever what a privilege it was for me to have spent so many hours with these intelligent and dedicated people. Dr. Ted was the eleven-year-old son of Dr. Fritsche, the much loved and respected mayor of New Ulm during World War I. Without the sharing of memories, as well as documentation, of those war years, *A Long Year of Silence* would not have the authenticity that I hope the story conveys.

Appreciation to Wallace Alwin for the time he gave to be interviewed in his home, while the ladies of the New Ulm Methodist church were baking Christmas cookies!

Thank you, Ellen Hawley, whose editing of my manuscript was most interesting, helpful and gently delivered.

And special thanks to Daniel Hoisington, publisher, Edinborough Press, for his encouragement and belief in my story. It has given me new life, in this, my eighth decade!

Most of all, appreciation for Fred, my husband and best friend, for his listening ear, excellent advice and unwavering support; and to Kristy, my daughter, for her patience during the birth pangs of this book!

Danke Schön, all of you!

For
Christian and Anna Hohn
and
Ted and Lois Fritsche

All Americans are either immigrants or
descendants of immigrants and ultimately
therefore a hyphenated American.
I am writing this story for them as well as
for my children, grandchildren, and great-
grandchildren, who also are descended
from German immigrants.

This is a story then for all Americans.

CHAPTER ONE

A Long, Sad Day

I WRAPPED MY ARMS around my books and hugged them close to me for comfort. I needed something real and solid to cling to as I hurried down the hall to Mr. Klemm's American history class, the last of this long, sad, upsetting day.

But much as I loved the way Mr. Klemm made the history of the United States jump with excitement, I didn't think I could stand sitting through one more hour of school. I had to at least catch a glimpse of Rudi, my secret friend—my first true love. I longed to search his face to see how he was taking the news, have a word with him and then rush home. I needed to reassure myself that my father's depression had lifted a little since we first learned the news headlined by every newspaper in the country:

WAR! UNITED STATES DECLARES WAR ON GERMANY!

This morning, that proclamation crashed down the halls and into the classrooms of New Ulm High School. He had made his choice. Just three days ago, on Good Friday, April 6, 1917, President Wilson announced to the nation that we were at war. From this day on, it was no longer England that many thought for so long was the enemy, but Germany. And Germany was *Heimatland*, homeland, of most of the people of New Ulm, Minnesota. And of my father, Christian Altenberg, minister of the town's German Methodist Church.

Just yesterday, Easter Sunday, Father stood in the pulpit in his long, black frock coat to lead the congregation in singing, "Alleluja! Christ has risen!" But he looked so sad, so defeated, with the weight of the world on his drooping shoulders, that none of us in the congregation seemed to be able to open our mouths, much less sing. I watched my father try to straighten up to his full six foot-two, and sound out louder in his deep, bass voice. Listening to him, seeing him try so hard, my own heart sank. Nobody in the entire congregation would believe Christ had risen!

My father's congregation had been pretty much all of one mind about our entering into a European conflict, but for months and months, the rest of the town had been divided about the war, half for it, half against it. So what had been such a peaceful, prosperous German-American community, now seemed to have a war going on inside it.

It had been getting more and more unpleasant. The declaration of war could only make it worse, I was sure. That's why I dreaded coming to school this morning. Like the town, half my classmates were for the war, half against it.

For myself, I wanted to be a part of both halves, but I just couldn't figure out what I thought or felt about any of it, in spite of knowing beyond a shadow of a doubt which side my peace loving father was on. And I certainly couldn't tell him how torn apart I was. It would break his heart. I loved and admired him so much, I couldn't bear hurting him any further than he was already hurt.

So, much as I dreaded it, I came to school this morning. There was nowhere except school that I could see Rudi Meyerdorf. He lived in Goosetown on the Bohemian side of the railroad tracks. I lived on this side—worlds apart.

I propped my chin on my books, looked down at my feet and hurried down the hall to Mr. Klemm's room. I slid into my seat, got out my notebook and pretended I was pouring over our last assignment for him, an essay on "Why I Am Proud to Be An American." I hoped and prayed my favorite teacher would not say anything to add to my confusion.

I barely raised my head when Mr. Klemm walked into the room and stood behind his desk. He looked at each of us carefully, then closed his eyes, pressed his hands together, and pushed them under his chin.

After the rustling of students getting seated and shuffling papers was over, the room became very still. I knew from his posture as he stood before his class that Mr. Klemm was about to say something important. Early spring sunshine poured through the windows and touched his beautiful, blond hair. He opened his eyes. They were a soft blue, the color of forget-me-nots. I held my breath.

"As you all know, only too well, we are at war—with Germany," he began, slowly, carefully. "My parents came from Germany, as did most of the people of New Ulm. You know that, too. We still speak German at home. I love the language—the music—the stories my mother and father tell about the Old Country."

He paused, looking at each one of his students, making sure we were all listening before he went on. He continued, "But I am an American. All American, not German-American. *The time has come for the hyphen to go.* I was born here and this is my country. I want what is best for my country. If our President thinks we have to go to war—even with Germany—*I'll stand by the President.*"

There was a stir in the classroom, an intake of breath all around me. In spite of myself and all my Father believed, I started to rise in my seat and shout, "I'll stand by the President, right beside you, Mr. Klemm!"

But then, my mind clouded. I swallowed the words before they burst out and eased back down, relieved I had not made a fool of myself. My heart was pounding, aching. There was Father—so much against the war, any war, so proud of being German-American. I had almost betrayed him. If he knew how I felt—that part of me also wanted the hyphen to go, wanted to be all American, too, he would—I couldn't finish the thought before Mr. Klemm continued.

"I want to tell you, class, before you hear it elsewhere, that when school is out, I will enlist in the army and go wherever I am sent and do whatever I am asked to do. You have been a wonderful class and I shall miss you. But I want you to know that it is for you, too, that I am doing this. *So your world will be safe for democracy.*"

All of us in the class gasped, one gasp.

Mr. Klemm didn't wait for a response. He clasped his hands, and rubbing them together in a let's-get-to-work gesture, he announced in a firm, confident voice, "Now, class, let's get on with our study of American history and enjoy our last weeks together."

No one moved. It was like everyone in the room was paralyzed. I felt the silence all around me. Now, after all the arguing and growing bitterness, our favorite teacher was enlisting. The war was not a debate any longer. It was real.

Now, more than ever, I wanted to see Rudi, then leave school and get home. And after seeing Father, sensing how he was feeling by the look on his face, the slump of his shoulders, I would go upstairs into the privacy of my own room, shut the door and try to sort out the tangle inside me. My feeling for Rudi—Father's feelings—my own.

After what seemed like hours, the bell rang and half the class—those that had been for the war—scrambled out of their seats and flocked around Mr. Klemm, shaking his hands, thanking him for what he had said and was going to do. A few of the girls had tears in their eyes. I ached as I watched. I wanted to follow them, wanted to throw my arms around Mr. Klemm and thank him for all he had taught us, and for his courage. But I did nothing. Father wasn't there, of course, but it felt like he was standing beside me, pressing down on my shoulder to keep me glued to my seat.

I watched the other half of our class slowly rise, slowly gather their books and start to leave the classroom. My chest hurt from the tears I wouldn't let myself shed—tears of sorrow for Mr. Klemm, for my father—for myself. I covered my face with my hands and lowered my head down onto my desk. I couldn't help it. I felt all alone, cut off from all of my classmates, both halves, not belonging anywhere. A few of my friends patted my shoulder as they left the room, saying nothing.

When I felt sure almost all of them had left, I managed to lift my head, free myself from my desk, gather my books in my arms and leave, too. I lowered my head again and hurried down the hall. I didn't want to talk to or listen to one more person until I had seen Rudi. Maybe with Rudi, I would feel as though I belonged, somewhere, to someone.

I slowed down when I saw him, standing just where I knew he would be, taking his basketball shoes out of his locker. The sight of him, the strength in his arms and shoulders, his amazing dark hair, the smooth grace of his movements, filled my whole being with wonder. He has to be the handsomest, finest, most remarkable boy in the whole world, I thought, as I gazed at his back. And he chose flat-chested, unremarkable, book-worm me to help him with his grammar. Maybe he asked me because I'm so plain. He wouldn't be embarrassed to make mistakes in front of me. Or maybe it was because I play piano for the Glee Club he sings in and I'm just there after practice—a convenience.

Rudi turned from his locker just as I was passing by and greeted me with the barest of smiles. "After Glee Club tomorrow, Emma? Same as usual? I need your help now, more than ever."

"Oh, *ja*, Rudi, of course, I'll love it! I—I mean—I'm always happy to be of help. When I can."

"*Du bist ein gute Lehrerin,*" Rudi said, a small grin warming his troubled face a little. "You are a good teacher. You teach me, then I teach *Mutti*, my mother. She's learning. She can't keep speaking just German forever."

Time was running out. What could I say that would hold him there just another moment?

"How—how is she, Rudi, your mother? How is she taking the news?"

Rudi closed his locker with a bang and tossed his basketball shoes over his shoulder. The grin was gone and a dark frown clouded his face.

"*Schrecklich*, Emma. Dreadful. *Mutti* so against the war. Always war in Europe. Her husband, my father, killed by the Prussians, you know. And my brother Winfried so much for this war. Torn apart, my family. Leaves *Mutti unwirklich*. What is the word *auf* English? Confused. *Ja*, that's it, confused. Muddled in the head."

"*Es tut mir sehr leid*, Rudi. I'm very sorry."

Time had run out. The bell shrilled a warning for the close of school this long, *schrecklich* day.

"Tomorrow, then," Rudi said, turned and walked away.

I watched him stride down the hall, his basketball shoes dangling down his back.

Now I was alone again.

"Please, *lieber Gott*, dear God," I breathed as I watched him disappear. "Let him feel something special for me."

Then, like a cold wind, a question came. Where and how far could this friendship go? How long could I keep it from my father? What would my father say—or do—if he knew his German Methodist minister's daughter was in love with a *Catholic*—a Bohemian Catholic at that! It was all too much. I was muddled in the head like Rudi's mother—and in the heart, too. I needed to get home, fast!

But I didn't move fast enough to keep from being followed. Before I'd gone less than half a block a voice behind me called, "What's the hurry, Em! Wait for me!"

Victoria Becker! This was the first time in my life I didn't want to see her, in spite of my loneliness. My feelings were too strong, too jumbled up, even for my best friend.

I turned and saw Victoria, waving and smiling, tripping along, trying to catch up with me. Even when she ran, her skirt swirling around her ankles, Victoria was graceful and beautiful. Tied with a blue satin ribbon, her fine-spun golden hair bounced against her shoulders. All those turnings, those gymnastics at the Turnverein, of course. And her bosom—so *there*—and mine? I hugged my books closer to me to hide my nothingness.

I pushed down a nubbin of irritation that poked at me. My best friend had been irritating me often lately. But never as much as in this moment. Seemed like that time of month Mama called the "dark of the moon" was with me all the time. I was changing, and it scared me. So I made myself smile and keep on smiling until Victoria caught up with me.

"Well, for pity's sake, Em," she chirped. "You've been so glum today. You've hardly said hello. I bet it's the war. Our boys having to fight overseas, maybe even killing their own relatives. Pater says that won't happen."

Victoria put her arm around my waist as we walked and the nubbin of irritation inside me grew stronger. She calls her father Pater, as if Latin was a second language. And she calls her elegant mother by her first name, Rosa. So pretentious to speak of one's parents that way!

Victoria went right on, patting my arm as she talked. "Pater says Wilson said we have no quarrel with the German people, and anyway—even if we have declared war on Germany, Wilson won't make German boys go overseas to fight their relatives. Pater and Mayor Fritsche and some others have gone to Washington to talk to President Wilson. He'll understand how we feel, for sure."

"I need to get home, Victoria." There was a testiness in my voice, I knew, something that had never been there before in all the long years Victoria and I had been friends. I started to walk faster to get away from her, but Victoria quickened her pace as she walked along beside me in silence. Silence was not something Victoria and I shared very often.

It was Victoria who broke the silence, her voice softer, "Lots of people are troubled, Em," she said, "now that we are actually at war. But you're taking it so—so personally. What's really the matter, kiddo?"

I stopped walking and looked at Vicky. This was my friend, my best friend, my secret-sharer. I had to tell her something, even though my head pounded and my heart ached and I needed to get home.

"I can't explain it, Vicky," I said, "But—I'm—I'm so—torn apart! Part of me wants to be fully American, not a hyphenated one. But then, there's Father. You know how he feels."

Victoria stopped, took her arm from around my waist and looked straight at me. "Of course I know how your father feels. Same as mine. But it's more than your father's feelings about the war, isn't it, kiddo? I know you too well. It's Rudi. Rudi Meyerdorf. Those English lessons you're supposed to be giving him—they've turned into something more, haven't they? And you don't want your father to know."

There was both hope and glee in her voice. How could she be so gleeful about something that was tormenting me?

"No, Vicky," I practically shouted, "It's not Rudi, really. Nothing is going on between Rudi and me. Believe me. He only thinks of me as his tutor."

"Come on, Em. Really, now. Why do you think he chose you to help him?"

"Well, I'm there, you know, playing piano for the Glee Club. And Mama knows his mother, too, so maybe he . . ."

"—thinks you're just a convenience," Vicky announced, finishing my sentence for me. "And because you're pretty and gentle and smart besides doesn't have anything to do with it? Come on, now, Emma Altenberg. Have you looked in the mirror ever?"

"I—I guess I have—I mean, *ja*, I have—I do. But Vicky, I'm so plain! So flat chested. What could he—"

"See in you, Emma? Now stop that! If you can't see yourself—perfect nose and blue eyes like a movie star, why I—. Anyway, I don't believe you. You have to know how pretty you are. Rudi has to have feelings for you—and you for him. You're just not being honest with me."

"I am, Vicky, for true. Cross my heart!"

"Well, if that's the case and you don't want him, I tell you, I'll take him. He's got to be the most—"

That did it! All the pain and confusion and fear of the day shoved the words right out of my mouth.

"You stop that, Victoria Becker! You're the biggest flirt in the whole school, making goo-goo eyes at all the boys. It's not Rudi Meyerdorf. It isn't! It's just that my father . . ."

"Hey, Em! Calm down, kiddo. If it's not Rudi, if it's really your father, Emma Altenberg, you worry too much about him. He's a grown man. Let your mother worry about him."

The nubbin of irritation inside me was suddenly a poker, hot as fire, and I heard myself spit out, "What do you know about my mother, Victoria Becker! All she thinks about is the Women's Christian Temperance Union! How much do you know about my father, either? How much do you really know about anything? Just because you're one of those free-thinking Turners and can think anything you want, doesn't mean somebody isn't right and somebody isn't wrong. You just think you know everything!"

I glared at Victoria. I couldn't believe what I heard in my voice. What was happening to me? Vicky's cheeriness was gone. Tears glimmered in her eyes. This was the first time I'd seen Victoria's tears in ages.

When she began to speak again, it was almost in a whisper, "Em—Em—I was only trying to help."

"That's another thing, Victoria Becker!" I heard myself going on and on. "I'm sick and tired of you helping me. I don't like you helping me all the time, anymore. I don't like it a bit!"

Victoria looked at me as though I'd hit her. Her face crumpled totally, her beautiful face. "I'm—I'm sorry, Em. It's just my big mouth. I'm upset, too. Pater and Rosa are upset. Everybody is upset these days—about the war, I mean. One way or the other."

My anger was crumpling fast as I looked at Vicky struggling to bring back her cheeriness.

"Talk to your father about your feelings, Emma. He's not God, you know."

Vicky carefully wiped the glistening tears that still brimmed in her eyes, gave me a brief hug and a half smile. I watched my friend turn and walk away toward her big, red brick house on German Street. Her step was slow. The bounce was gone. How could I be so mean, I wondered, shocked and shamed at the strength of my outburst. Where was all this coming from? Victoria was my chance to feel close to someone, as though I belonged. And here I was, turning her away. Was this what the war was doing to me?

"Vicky! Vicky," I called to the disappearing figure, "I'm sorry, too!"

Victoria stopped, waved, then rounded the corner and disappeared.

I looked down the empty street, then turned and walked on toward the parsonage, my own small home, needing to get there, yet dreading it. Talk to your father, Vicky had said. She didn't have any idea how impossible that seemed to me.

I pictured my home now, with Mama bustling and sputtering to herself in the kitchen and Father shut up in his study that Mama called his "Holy of Holies." He'd be working hard on next Sunday's sermon, I was sure, struggling to say the right thing about peace on earth. I couldn't imagine telling him how I often felt about longing to be all American—and certainly not about Rudi. I hadn't even told Father and Mama I'd been seeing Rudi, alone for tutoring after school, for weeks. The longer I waited, the harder it was getting to be.

And why had I hid the truth from Victoria? I never had in the past. Didn't I trust her—my best friend? Maybe it was because there really wasn't anything to tell—yet. Maybe because it was something I wanted to keep all to myself, like the little things I'd kept in my treasure box since I was a little child. It was Indian-made, of birch bark, decorated with porcupine quills and was my most loved possession. It held treasures given to me by people I loved, reminding me of times I never wanted to forget. I wondered now, if I would ever have something from Rudi to put inside?

So many strange, overwhelming thoughts and feelings this sad, unreal, lonely day. Rudi had used a word, a strong, resounding German word—*schrecklich*—dreadful.

I walked on home, slowly now, still clutching my books.

CHAPTER TWO

War Inside Our Walls

THE SOUND OF rattling pans and the cinnamon fragrance of *apfel kuchen* and freshly brewed coffee filled my nose the moment I stepped into the house. Mama was baking. That meant we were having company. No surprise. The parsonage was the church office, church parlor and pastor's study for our little church next door and Mama's hot coffee was part of almost every gathering. "Coffee and love are best when hot," Mama would often say, in German, chuckling to herself, her cheeks turning pink. I wasn't sure I knew exactly what that meant.

Not only deacons and board members came to discuss church business, but men from the whole community met here often to discuss every weighty thing from religion and politics to the progress of the crops on the farm. Sometimes, I thought the whole town loved to come and talk to Father. The Jewish people had no temple or synagogue, so they would call Father, asking if the "rabbi" was in. They said he had a "Talmudic mind," whatever that meant. Father loved that. This afternoon some of the men surely would be gathering to discuss the day's disturbing news.

It was all so familiar. Maybe this, after all, was where I really belonged. On my way to the kitchen, I passed the Holy of Holies. The door was closed and deep men's voices rumbled from inside. They sounded tense, but sprinkled with small ripples of laughter and a *"gut—gut."* Good, good, they were saying. My spirits lifted a little. Whatever was going on inside couldn't be all gloom.

Mama was bustling about in the kitchen, taking an *apfel kuchen* out of the oven. I kissed her on the cheek and dropped my books on the kitchen table.

11

"*Nein!* No, Emma," Mama said. "Pick up your books! I need the table."

The same irritation I'd felt with Victoria poked at my stomach. Why did Mama rub me the wrong way all the time? Everyone in town is kitchen comfortable with Mama. Except me. We're so different. She's so round. Plump, really. Jolly, everybody says. I'm so—so—I don't know what I am anymore.

But I did as I was told, picked up my books and went upstairs. This was no time to fuss with Mama.

When I came back downstairs the men still hadn't left and it seemed to take forever for the them to come out of Father's study, have their coffee and say *"Auf Wiedersehen."*

The last good-bye finally was said. Father closed the front door and opened the door to his study.

"Nasty smell," Mama sputtered as she flicked her dish towel up and down trying to rid the parlor of tobacco fumes still in the air.

Father started to pick up plates and cups and carry them to the kitchen. He looked like he was going through a ritual he had performed many times and didn't need to think about what he was doing. His mind was clearly somewhere else, thinking of other things.

"*Wie geht's, Vater.* How goes it with you?" I finally said, afraid if I didn't say something, he would bump into me and drop the dishes he was carrying.

Father started at the sound of my voice, then looked at me, smiled warmly, but faintly. "*Meine Tochter*, my Emmeline, you're home," he said.

"*Ja*, Father, I'm home. It's been a long day, but I'm home!"

"*Ach so*, Emma, A long day indeed. How did things go at school?"

"Not easy, Father. So much tension. After all the talking and arguing that's been going on, it got real quiet—some talking, but mostly just silence—even in the halls."

Father looked at me as though from distance, then slowly shook his head. "The dye is cast. I hoped and prayed the good Lord would spare us war with our homeland. But perhaps the rally we're planning—our effort to keep drafted men here at home doing something for their country—will be successful. We must have faith."

A feeling of dread came over me. I'd have to tell him about Mr. Klemm. He would hear about it soon enough. The news will get around town. Mr. Klemm is the most influential teacher in the whole school. He'll be an example. He'll inspire lots of others to enlist, even before they're drafted. Father will be dismayed.

"Mr. Klemm is going to enlist as soon as school is out," I blurted out.

Father stared at me, stunned. He didn't speak for a long time. Then, he shook his head again and in a voice so low and far away I could barely hear him, he said, "War is such a waste. Young lives sacrificed. We elders make the wars then send the young to do the fighting—and dying."

Until this moment, I hadn't thought enlisting might mean dying! Enlisting was bad enough. But dying?" I shuddered.

"But *komm*, Emma, come," Father said, interrupting my awful thoughts, "we help your mother clear the dishes. We pray the good Lord will protect Mr. Klemm. A fine young man. Now we must pray our rally will be successful. That the President and Congress will hear us and not send our young men overseas to fight their loved ones."

He set down the dishes he still absently held, drew my head against his shoulder and cupped his warm hand against my cheek. "We must have faith, *liebchen*," he said again, and then started for the kitchen to help Mama.

"It's the mothers that give their sons to the war," Mama fussed, rising from the table that evening to fill Father's coffee cup, or add more schnitzel beans to the empty dish. "And how much credit do they get for that?"

"*Ja*, Mama," Father answered, calmly. "So true." That's all he said. His thoughts seemed to be far away.

Mama went right on, used to Father's absent-mindedness. "Seems to me we have enough problems of our own right here in this country without getting mixed up in foreign affairs. Drinking, for instance. There ought to be a law."

"Maybe so," Father said, absent still.

My mind drifted, too. I was back at school, hearing Mr. Klemm's announcement, the divided feelings about the war among all my classmates, my feelings of aloneness, my meanness with Vicky. I was especially thinking about Rudi. I'd see him tomorrow. Some brightness on the horizon, anyway. Mama was going right on, not seeming to care if she was heard or not.

"And I'm worried about the Grossbach's and about Frau Meyerdorf. She's a widow. And her youngest son is such a problem. If Rudi should be drafted—what would she do?"

Suddenly, I was fully present. Was Mama reading my mind? A chill rushed through me. Rudi! Drafted! Gone from New Ulm? Fighting? Dying? This was much worse than Mr. Klemm.

"He's—he's not old enough," I heard myself say, all in a rush. "He's only seventeen. A junior. Seems older because he's so responsible. His father died in Bohemia before they came here, you know."

Instead of stopping, as part of me knew I should, I found myself talking faster and saying more and more. I ran on and on, telling my parents things they surely already knew, as though I were defending Rudi. As though he needed defending.

"The Meyerdorfs had such a hard time in Bohemia, you know. Rudi's aunt thought they would do better here. Education for Rudi and Winfried, you know. And Frau Meyerdorf could raise geese and make feather pillows—and—lace things. And sell them."

My voice faded. I knew I had gone too far, said too much.

Both Father and Mama gazed at me in surprise. "And he's so talented. In music," I added lamely.

Father didn't say anything. Mama went right on with her questioning. "How come you're so interested and know so much about Rudi, Emma?"

"Well, I—you know, I play piano for the boy's Glee Club. And he's in it, you know. Sings just beautiful and plays every instrument there is. Everybody knows Rudi."

Father was still looking at me, a puzzled frown on his face, saying nothing.

Mama went right on. "But how did you learn about his father, Emma? I've visited Frau Meyerdorf many times. In Goosetown. Bought feather pillows from her. Watched her making her beautiful lace on her *Klöppelsack*. She's never talked about her husband. Never talked about the past—only about her pride in Rudi and her worry about her Winfried."

"Well, I—" All at once, the atmosphere felt like the inquisition. I squirmed in my seat. Why did I keep postponing telling them the truth—that I had new, deep, mysterious feelings for a boy—a handsome, dark-eyed, curly haired junior in High School who was a Bohemian, a musician, and like a gypsy, played the mandolin and zither in beer halls and saloons, lived in Goosetown—and was Catholic!

Father's steady gaze chilled me to the bone. "Emma, we know you are getting old enough to be interested in young men. But much as you may admire Rudi Meyerdorf, just remember that he is Catholic. You must not get too close, too serious with him. *Verstehts du?* Do you understand?"

He didn't wait for me to answer, but stood up, smiled at me briefly and left the room.

"*Ja, Vater,*" I said to myself, "*Ich verstehe.* I understand." But I didn't.

Mama shook her head and got up, too, and headed for the kitchen.

I sat at the table by myself, feeling alone again, and bewildered. Why had I even mentioned Rudi? Strange. Now I felt as though I had betrayed him, somehow—betrayed a friendship that was different and frightening and more wonderful than any I had ever known. Would Father's solemn warning change everything? Would I look at Rudi tomorrow, and not see him, wonderful Rudi Meyerdorf, but *Catholic* written all over his face? There was no place I could go to try and sort it all out, except upstairs to the silence of my own room, which I did, without helping Mama with the dishes. And for once, Mama didn't call me back down. *Gott sei dank!* Thank the Lord.

CHAPTER THREE

Too Close, Too Personal

"EMMA, YOU HAVEN'T said anything. What do you think?"

Max Brauer's voice came to me as though from a distance. I blinked, trying to get his face into focus and bring my mind into the library, the before school meeting place for our school paper, the *Graphos*. Max, our editor, stood at the table in the library, looking down at me with a faint smile on his face. The other ten members of the school paper staff sitting around me were looking at me, waiting for my response. I felt my cheeks grow warm.

"Uh—what? What did you say?"

"Speak up. This is important. What should go in this edition, now that we are at war?"

"Well, I think—" I began, and looked up at the clock. A quarter to nine. Fifteen more minutes of *Graphos* staff meeting and then seven more hours until I could see Rudi.

"I think . . . ," I began again, groping for something to say, "I think somebody should interview Mr. Klemm." There, I'd spoken up.

"Good idea, Emma," Walter Ebers, who was sitting next to me said. "You do the interview."

"Oh no, please, Walter, not that. I'll do anything. I'll edit the student entries in the *Graphos* box. I'll write up the Glee Club, the Daughters of Thespis, review their plays, things like that. Anything but Mr. Klemm."

"Why not?" Walter persisted, a dark scowl on his face. "You think people shouldn't enlist? You think we shouldn't be in this war?"

Not another argument, I thought with dismay. I didn't think I could stand it. I'd tossed and turned all night, worrying about Father and

16

Rudi and Victoria and the war and I was so tired I could hardly see, much less think.

I felt a warm hand covering mine, Amelia's. Amelia Grossbach was sitting beside me. She and her brother Karl were my best friends, next to Victoria. They were so close we called each others parents aunt and uncle, *Tante* and *Onkel*. The Grossbachs felt about the war just as Father did, which was just the opposite of Walter Ebers.

Amelia's reassuring touch cleared the confusion in my mind just enough for a thought to form. "No, please, it's not that. Really. It's just that I don't do interviews well," I said, and held my breath. I couldn't tell him I was too confused to write anything.

"You should do it," Walter persisted. "Show your patriotism."

A fist pounded on the table. It was Max. "Leave her alone, Walter Ebers. You're not the editor of this paper. I am!"

"And you're not our faculty advisor, Max Brauer," Walter shouted. "You're just one of us. And it's plain you're on Emma's side in this thing. You're both against this war! You're both—"

Seven boys were on their feet, all talking at once, interrupting each other, getting louder and louder, no one listening to anyone.

"Max—Walter—please." It was Bertha Brinkman. Bertha, Amelia, Katrin, Anneke, and myself, the only girls on the staff, were the only ones still seated. Bertha's hands covered her ears. She rarely spoke, but when she did, everyone listened. She and Max were sweet on each other, I knew. Maybe she would bring a more peaceful spirit into the room.

"Listen," Bertha went on. "Please! Let's try and get along. We've been arguing and shouting at each other for months now. Our whole town is torn apart. We have to think of something to bring us together. Now that we are at war—with Germany."

The boys quieted down, although Walter scraped his chair angrily as he pulled it up to the library table, grumbling to himself, but saying nothing.

"Well, I think we should have our faculty advisor sit in on these meetings," Louis Snyder grumbled. "Every meeting we've had all year has ended in a fight."

"Emma," Max said, somewhat calmer now, ignoring Louis, "Why don't you write up the All-School Picnic then. And the Prom?"

"And I'll interview Mr. Klemm," Bertha said, looking at me with a smile.

"*Danke schön*, thank you," I answered.

"I think we should stop using German all the time," Paul Weber snapped.

The bell rang before another argument got started. I closed my eyes with relief. Seven more hours to live through before the magic time with Rudi.

The rest of the day dragged on. I'd been so upset the night before, I hadn't finished my geometry assignment. Just before math class I saw Karl Grossbach, coming toward me in long legged strides, a twiggy tuft of hair sticking up at the back of his head. He was taller than Father, but in spite of his height I always saw him as the grave little boy I used to run around his father's farm with when we were children. He's the one I often asked for math help. But he was a grown man now and would be graduating in May.

Karl had started to school later than most and was so quiet some people thought he was just an average, gangly farm boy. But his brilliance in math as well as his quiet strength soon made him stand out among all of the other boys in the senior class. I was proud of both Karl and Amelia.

He stopped when he saw me and put his hand on my shoulder. Lately there had been a soft, searching look in his eyes when he looked at me. I wasn't sure what it meant and wasn't sure I liked it. He had always been my only brother and I wanted it to stay that way forever.

"Did Amelia talk to you this morning, Emma?" he asked. "At the *Graphos* meeting?"

"She didn't have a chance, Karl. We had another one of our arguments, you know."

"*Ja*, so. It goes on and on. But we needed to ask you—tell your father, your mother, too, that *Grossmutter, Oma*, needs to see him. She's upset something terrible. This war, you know. She's taken to her bed and we worry so. We need to see you, as soon as you can make it. I told mother we'd ask. Can you come soon, do you think? *Bitte?* Please?"

Never before had I heard such urgency in Karl's voice. My unfinished geometry was forgotten.

"Oh, Karl, of course. I'll tell Father. You know we'll come. You're family, Karl."

"*Ja*, sure, Emma. *Danke*," he answered and tried to smile before he turned to go.

I sat through geometry and then Mr. Klemm's class. Karl's distress haunted me. Everything that happened since yesterday seemed so unreal. I stared at Mr. Klemm, trying to keep my mind on what he said about the Spanish-American War, and all that the men of New Ulm had done for our country then. But I pictured him in a trench, bloody and dying.

When at last the bell shrilled the end of the school day, I swept up my books, hurried out of the room and down the hall to Glee Club practice. I needed to see Rudi. I needed to see if he was real.

I slipped into my place on the piano bench, spread out my music and looked up over the top of our bright, new Fisher Upright piano to the tenor section of the Glee Club. There he was, standing straight and tall, eyes focused gravely on Miss Schmidt, our director. The moment I saw him, I knew. I didn't see *Catholic*. I saw Rudi, Rudi Meyerdorf, the most handsome, caring, talented boy in the whole world. And I knew I loved him, Catholic or no Catholic. If only I knew how he felt about me.

I managed to pull my eyes away from Rudi's just in time to see Miss Schmidt raise her baton and look over at me to see if I was ready. I raised my fingers above those familiar ivory keys. For an instant both my hands felt unmovable, stiff and cold, the music on the sheet in front of me blurred. Then, the nod from Miss Schmidt, and the downward thrust of her baton and the musician in me came alive and stayed alive all during practice. I don't know how I did it, but I didn't want to let Miss Schmidt down, and certainly didn't want to embarrass myself in front of Rudi. And I loved the music and the sound of those beautiful male voices.

When practice was finished for the day and the Glee Club was dismissed, all of the boys, except Rudi, scrambled out of the room. Miss Schmidt gathered up her music and followed them. Just as she reached the door, she stopped, looked back at us, smiled, wiggled her fingers in a little wave and softly closed the door.

Rudi and I were alone. He looked at me gravely, started to move toward me. Stopped. My heart pounded.

"You play just beautiful, Emma," he said.

I smiled and hoped my trembling didn't show. Should I remind him now, that in English you need an adverb to describe a verb. You needed to say "You play beautifully." Would I be too teacherish and spoil what might be happening? I knew Vicky was right. Boys didn't like girls to be too smart. It was bad enough being his tutor.

"Thank you, Rudi," I managed to say. "Should we look at the book? I always forget to use adverbs, too. And I always end sentences with prepositions like 'will you come with.'"

I was sure my shaky little laugh sounded silly.

Rudi smiled weakly and we sat down, side by side, not touching, and opened our grammar books. I tried to concentrate on the lesson and explain things as best I could without sounding like I knew everything.

At the end of the session, Rudi closed his grammar book with a snap. It sounded so final, like the end of our times together. My heart sank. Maybe I had hurt his feelings. Maybe I had sounded too smart.

"Emma Louise," he said, going back to his familiar German, "I have to say, I admire you very much—you—your whole family. Thank you for helping me."

My mind reeled. He admires me, his tutor. He admires my whole family. Is this all? *Lieber Gott,* dear God, don't let this be the end!

Forcing a smile, I managed to answer as casually as I could, "I was happy to try. You are using more and better English all the time."

The bell sounded its dismal warning again. Time had run out. This was it for another day.

"Well, you see, Emma, what I was going to say—I must not go on with our lessons. There is so much I must do. Basketball practice for the tournament and more practices with the Hofmeister band, you know, getting ready for the summer parades—the Fourth of July parade—the big rally later. I play trumpet, you know."

Keep smiling, Emma. Keep casual. He mustn't know how you really feel, I scolded myself.

Aloud I managed to say, "*Ja,* I know. We're proud of you, being in Hofmeister's band and all."

"*Danke schön.* Thank you. Hofmeister's Band is the best thing I do, but I need to play guitar weekends to help with the money at home. In *Bier Gartens,* I play—places like that. This war hasn't changed everything—yet." He sounded apologetic. My family's Methodist reputation for prohibition had gotten around, for sure.

"Oh, I understand!" I answered, quickly.

"Well, then," he went on, "I guess you are pretty busy, too?"

Was I imagining he was trying to keep the conversation going? Warmth poured through me, lovely as the spring sunshine that filled the room.

"I—well," I said, groping for words to make my life sound interesting. "I help Mama at home during the week, and of course, Sundays there's always church. In the morning. And evening, too." I smiled as brightly as I could. "We have prayer meetings Wednesday nights, but I don't have to go to those," I added, not sure why.

"It must sometimes be hard. Being a minister's daughter, *nicht wahr?* Not so? We have priests and they don't marry."

"Maybe that's wise," I said, the thought occurring to me for the first time, thinking of Father, how busy he was with church affairs. Gone so much. Locked up in his "Holy of Holies."

"Do you go to the parades, ever? Like the Fourth of July?"

"Oh, *ja*, we do. We do! The Methodists have a picnic Fourth of July, always. Baseball games, things like that. But we go to parades, too."

"You'll be playing piano for Glee Club next year?"

"I expect to. You'll be singing?"

"I think. But I'm not sure. I am too busy all the time. I have to make some choices. But that's next year. Far away. You'll be at the Junior-Senior prom, maybe? Serving our dinner?"

"Oh, *ja*. I'll be there serving dinner. I have to write it up for the *Graphos*, too."

"Well, then, I see you there, and maybe sometime this summer. Until then, *wiedersehen*." He turned abruptly and hurried down the hall.

It was over. Our time together had ended, I realized with a heavy heart. My chance of seeing Rudi except from a distance until September were slim. Our worlds were so far apart for sure, even though we lived in the same town. During the summer, he'd forget all about me and in the fall, he'd be a Senior and me a lowly Junior. He'd be too busy to continue our English lessons. He might even be too busy to be in the Glee Club. Even though I thought my feelings were one-sided, seeing him every week alone had given me some hope.

I slowly gathered my music, filled my arms with books and left the music room. All hope was gone.

A voice called to me from down the hall. Rudi's voice!

"Emma, Emma Altenberg! I just remembered the All-School Picnic! Will you come with?"

Forget the grammar! Forget Mama and Father! Forget Bohemian-German, playing in saloons—forget *Catholic!*

"*Ja*, oh *ja*, Rudi! I maybe can't come with, but I'll meet you there!"

"*Gut*, Emma, good. The picnic, then. I'll see you in Hermann Heights somewhere!"

Joy rose inside me like a bird released from a cage. He wants to be with me! It's like Christmas and birthday and the resurrection all in one! I wanted to run, to skip, to shout out loud. Oh joy!

It would be weeks before the picnic, I said to myself on the way home. But I'd keep busy. I'd look up some history of Hermann the Great before standing beneath that awesome statue at the All-School picnic. I'd never really liked Hermann, the German, but maybe I'd get an idea for my essay on why I was proud to be an American. And I'd be working on the High School annual and I'd be helping serve dinner at the Junior-Senior Prom—"

I stopped in my tracks. The Junior-Senior Prom! Rudi would be there. He'd be out on the dance floor after the banquet, dancing. Dancing with every Junior and Senior girl in our High School. And I couldn't dance. I didn't know how. I wasn't allowed to learn.

I shivered in spite of the spring sunshine that warmed my back and hurried home. Methodists don't believe in dancing. A dark, tight feeling started crowding out the hope and joy I had felt just a minute before. I didn't run. I didn't skip. I dragged myself home to the Methodist parsonage. It must be hard, sometimes, being a minister's daughter. Rudi had said. Oh, Rudi, how right you are!

CHAPTER FOUR

Ich Will Frieden!

"OMA GROSSBACH MAY never again be able to come to church, so I take communion to her," Father announced after breakfast the following Saturday. "I've finished my sermon. Such a beautiful day it is. The roads are dry. We all go, *ja*?"

"Oh, *ja*, we all go," Mama said, jumping up from the table." It will do us all good to get out into the country and bring a little cheer to Oma. Come, Emma, help me make *ranzes*. The Grossbachs love them so much."

I bustled about the kitchen, trying to keep up with Mama, eager to get out of the house and into the spring sunshine. Maybe driving through the open countryside with my parents, would take my mind off all my troubles—Rudi, the upcoming Prom, Mr. Klemm, the war. And maybe Father's spirits would lighten and lift the tension in the air all around us. Father would be doing something for little Oma and he loved doing things for people. Best of all, he loved the farm.

With every mile out of town, into the country, the war seemed further away. We passed fields of black, moist earth, freed from the blanket of snow that had covered them for so many months. The fragrance of spring rose from the ditches and mingled with the comforting smell of the ranzes, the cabbage and hamburger filled buns Mama made and I packed.

"This country reminds me, very nearly, of Germany," Father said as our Ford car rumbled along the bumpy road. "The hills were higher there, but the trees, some of the birds and wildflowers are the same."

"Did you have wild plums and choke cherries in Germany, like here, Father?" I asked breathing in the fresh country air. "I'll remember forever how you set me on your shoulders to pick the fruit from the trees when I was just a little girl."

"Oh, *ja*," Father answered, "Wild strawberries, *Erdbeeren*, we had, too, and we made wine from wild grapes."

"Oh no!" said Mama, always alarmed at any mention of alcoholic beverages.

"Well, we didn't have good water to drink, so we drank wine. In moderation, *natürlich*, naturally."

"I miss our little mare clopping along with barely enough strength to pull our buggy," Mama said, quickly changing the subject.

"But we get there faster in the Ford car," I shouted over the rumble of our automobile. "Look. We're here already."

"Dietrich has some work to do. Snow pushed his mailbox almost over," Father said as they approached the rutted lane leading into the Grossbach's farm yard.

"He'll get at it," Mama said. "He's a worker, that Dietrich. They all are."

We had barely stepped out of the car when the whole Grossbach family came out to greet us. All except Oma. "Oh, you shouldn't have," Tante said as she took the basket of lunch from Mama's hand.

Karl came up to me with a warm smile. "*Kommst du mit,* you want to come with? I go mend a fence so the cows won't tromp on the fields when we start to plant."

"Oh, Karl," I surprised myself by saying. "I—I don't have my knickers on. And—and I promised to play piano for Father when he sings for Oma."

I couldn't quite understand my hesitation this day, but it had something to do with the searching look on Karl's face lately. And something to do with Rudi, maybe?

"So *geht's*," Karl said, soberly, a bewildered look on his face. "So it goes. Another time. When the wild flowers are in bloom, *ja*?" He turned quickly and walked away, his two little brothers, Franz and Hubert, following him like trusting puppies. A gentle breeze lifted his blond tuft of hair just a little.

A strange sadness came over me as I watched Karl stride toward the meadow, as though I were saying good-bye to our childhood. Since the day war was declared, everything seemed to be changing. Me, especially.

Inside the sparkling clean farmhouse, Onkel Grossbach carried little Oma from her bedroom into the parlor, next to the piano. He tucked her fragile frame into their one big chair. Tante, Amelia, and Mama gathered round on straight chairs from the kitchen. Onkel sat on the arm of Oma's chair and I sat at the piano to play for Father. It seemed to me that every German family had a piano, even if they didn't have a couch.

When Father finished singing, *"Ich bete an die Macht der Liebe,"* Oma took Father's long-fingered hand in both her tiny withered ones and pressed it to her cheek. Soft sobs shook her trembling body.

"Oh, my dear Pastor Christian," she managed to gasp, all in German, because she knew no English, "will my dear grandson Karl have to fight the family we left in Germany?"

Before Father had a chance to answer Oma, Onkel Dietrich broke in. "I didn't come to this country to have my sons go to war," he said, his face reddening like a sun burn in summer. "I left the Old Country to get away from war," he went on. "They war all the time over there. Never stop. And the Kaiser keeps building tanks and submarines and leaves the poor, poor yet. So we come here. It was hard. But we come. And we work. *Arbeit und arbeit."*

I held my breath. This was an Onkel Dietrich I had never seen before.

"Ich will Frieden! I want peace! I will not let my sons go to war. I will not have them be cannon fodder!" he shouted, in a voice that didn't have a shred of peace in it. "I want my sons to live and help me farm!"

And with that he turned and left the room.

No one spoke. Oma stopped her weeping and shook her head silently for a long time. When she began to speak, it was in a raspy whisper.

"I worry so about Dietrich. We worry about my brothers and sisters in Germany. Now that we are at war—"

She could go no further. She laid her head against the back of the chair and closed her eyes. I thought Oma must be breathing her last and wondered with aching heart why no one moved. It was Father who broke the silence. I watched him walk over to the tiny, grieving old woman, kneel in front of her chair and take her hands tenderly in his own.

"*Liebe Oma*, you must not worry and grieve so much. Some town leaders are supporting a petition asking that the President and Congress not force our German-American sons to go overseas to fight their friends and relations. Surely, President Wilson and Congress will listen. They'll find ways for our boys to serve their country here at home. We must have faith, Oma. Faith in God and in our President."

Oma lifted her head from the chair, opened her eyes and looked at Father, a gentle smile deepening a thousand wrinkles. "A petition that might save our sons from killing? That's good news, pastor! Maybe there is some hope, after all. This is a good country. We have a good President, I know."

The trust I saw in her eyes as she looked at Father brought tears to my eyes. "Bless you, pastor," she whispered as Tante and Mama and Amelia started to leave the room. "Pray with me now, will you—for peace?"

I looked back for a moment and saw Father still kneeling in front of Oma's chair, his long, tapering fingers folded in prayer.

"Dear God," I heard him begin in his deep bass voice, "with all our hearts this day, we pray for peace . . . ." I closed the door softly behind me.

It had been a sobering time, all of it, Onkel's outburst, Oma's grief, then hope returned. As I joined the women in the kitchen, I realized that for this last tense hour, I had forgotten all about Rudi Meyerdorf and having to watch him dance at the prom, and not being able to dance myself. I forgot about the arguments at school, my confusion about Mr. Klemm and being all American. All I felt was tenderness for the Grossbachs and pride in being my father's daughter.

Onkel Dietrich did not appear before we left and I saw nothing more of Karl or his little brothers. Silent embraces and 'wiedersehens' were all we exchanged with Tante and Amelia when we left their farmyard.

As we bumped along the dirt road toward home, silently watching the sun slide down the sky in lavender layers, Rudi slid into my mind again. And I remembered Karl disappearing towards the woods beyond the meadow, Frank and Hubert trailing after, not once looking back. I wondered if I would ever regret not going with him. I tried to imagine Rudi crossing the flower-filled meadow with me some spring and wondered if he would love it as I always had. Would I ever have a chance to find out?

As I was thinking, thinking about all I'd seen and felt at the Grossbachs, I guessed Mama and Father did the same. No need to talk about what had been so sobering.

So as we rode along silently, I tried to push it all out of my mind, concentrating instead on being with Rudi at the All-School Picnic in three more weeks.

CHAPTER FIVE

Watching the Dance

"I DON'T WANT to be here!" I felt like stomping my foot and running back home as I stood in front of the door to our high school gymnasium, looking down the hall at all the American flags flying there. It was the second week in May and still light—a sweet, balmy evening for the Junior-Senior Prom, 1917. When I thought about meeting Rudi at the All-School Picnic, I'd totally forgotten about the Prom. Purposely forgotten, I think.

I was about to open the door to the gym when I felt warm hands over my eyes and a whispery giggle in my ears. "Don't peek until you're in the gym, Em. You'll never believe it."

"Vicky, you scared me to death almost!"

"I know, but I want you to be surprised."

Vicky opened the door for us, one hand still covering my eyes. When she took her hand away, I gasped in wonderment. The whole room was literally covered with lavender and white ribbons, our school colors, running from the center of the ceiling to the walls in graceful curves. From the middle of the ceiling a dainty umbrella was hanging, red, white and blue ribbons fluttering from it. At opposite corners of the gym, beautifully decorated booths held bowls of frappe. Tables were set up for the dinner all around the edges of the room.

"See! Isn't it grand?" Vicky giggled, squeezing my arm. "The Juniors spent a whole week decorating. They want to make this as wonderful for the Seniors as they can, as if there were no war!"

I was too stunned to say anything as I watched the Juniors and Seniors, faculty members and school board members come pouring in. I saw Karl Grossbach come in, looking grave and uncomfortable in his stiff black suit. He smiled, waved at me and joined a group of boys standing by the frappe table. I looked around for Rudi, saw him, but he seemed to be having a good time, talking to a beautifully dressed Senior, a glass of frappe in their hands. He didn't seem to be looking for me. How could I possibly get through this night! I took a deep breath, swallowed and tried to fight back the tears with all my strength. It was Vicky who saved me.

"Come on, Em." Vicky said as she pulled me into the kitchen to put on our little aprons and frilly caps that were supposed to make us look like maids in a fancy restaurant. Thinking of the beautiful, silvery evening gown Rudi's Senior wore, my funny little outfit made me feel silly as a goose. I would avoid Rudi's seeing me, if I possibly could.

As we came back into the gym with our trays of fruit cocktail, a loud chord from the piano called everyone to attention and Stanley Offenbach, Junior class president called out, "See the umbrella up there? There's a ribbon with a name on it. Grab a ribbon, boys, and find your partner!"

There was a grand rush and the ribbons were gone. I watched Rudi grab a ribbon and held my breath to see who his partner would be. *Lieber Gott*, don't let it be the beautiful Senior!

"Can you believe that, Em?" Vicky whispered. "Rudi got Bertha Brinkman. Boy, oh boy, will Max ever be jealous!"

What could I say? I felt sorry for Max as he walked up to his partner, Frieda Hoch, surely not the prettiest or thinnest girl in the school. But he gallantly escorted her to a place next to him at a table. After all, he had no choice. And at least my fear that Rudi would pick the beautiful Senior's ribbon eased—at least during dinner.

We Sophomore girls and boys served the dinner quietly, trying to not call attention to ourselves, as we had been instructed. That was fine with me, and I managed not to have to serve Rudi. Being his tutor was bad enough—but his waitress—in a silly little outfit!

All during the meal the orchestra played and everyone kept time to the music with their knives and forks clinking against their glasses. Then, the tables were cleared and moved against the wall to make room for the dancing to begin. We waiters and waitresses leaned against the tables and watched the dancers as they moved eagerly onto the dance floor.

I held my breath as I watched Rudi take Bertha Brinkman into his arms, hold her close and whirl gracefully around the room. After the first dance, Max cut in and took Bertha into his own arms. I saw Karl leave the room. He was probably going into one of the rooms prepared for those who preferred to play games. Dear Karl, he couldn't dance either. I saw Rudi look around, find an unclaimed girl, then lead her confidently on to the dance floor.

"Look at that Rudi dance!" Vicky whispered in my ear. He's far and away the best dancer in the room."

"Oh, really?" I answered casually as Rudi danced with one partner after the other, holding them close and moving gracefully like birds in flight. I tried to turn away and fade into the kitchen, but I couldn't. I stayed glued to the sight of Rudi dancing, dancing with every Junior and Senior girl in the whole school, even chubby Frieda Hoch. At least he was considerate and he certainly loved to dance, but I could almost hear my heart break as I watched.

Shortly before midnight the orchestra started playing "Home Sweet Home" and our principal told everyone to say good-bye, the party was over, they must go straight home. There were murmurs of regret, a few tears, then everyone started to gather their wraps and leave. I wondered how many would go straight home. I wondered if Rudi would. I could hardly wait to go straight home. Just before hurrying to the kitchen, Karl came by, tapped me on the shoulder, said, "*Gute Nacht*, Emmeline," and left.

In the kitchen Victoria was putting on her cape.

"Stefan Schroeder is walking me home, Emma. Hope you don't mind," Vicky said.

"Of course not," I lied. They walked with me down the empty hall and left me to walk on alone.

Mama and Father, trusting me completely, left my light on and turned down my covers. I crawled into bed, turned off the little lamp and reached in the darkness for my treasure box. I fingered it now for comfort as I started my all-night staring into the darkness of the May night. The painful, painful memory of this night would stay with me forever. I was sure of it.

I had been to the Prom, and yet I had really not been there. I'd gone though the motions, done my part. But my sadness must be deeper than all the rest. Mr. Klemm would not be there next year. Karl would not. It would be Rudi's last year at New Ulm High School and we would probably never be partners at the Junior-Senior Prom. And I—daughter of a minister—would never in my life be able to dance with Rudi Meyerdorf.

Just as the soft grey of dawn crept into my room, more and more birds joined the earliest bird. It was just light enough for me to see the calendar on the wall, special dates circled. The All-School Picnic in two weeks was circled in red. One last chance. Rudi suggested that he meet me there. Maybe he would. I finally fell asleep.

CHAPTER SIX

Heights and Depths

THOSE TWO WEEKS dragged, in spite of all the things that needed to be done. Until this year I had always been on time with my assignments. This spring, though, my mind had been on so many things, I found my thoughts drifting out the windows of my classrooms and I completely forgot about my essay, "Why I Am Proud To Be An American." These last days of school I crammed to catch up. I hated the thought of bringing home a report card that was less than all A's. I hated to see the disappointment on Father's face. So I stayed up late, lost sleep, got Karl to help me with geometry and the days slowly crept by.

May 22 and the day of the All-School Picnic finally arrived. It was a perfect, cloudless day. We three Altenbergs drove up the long hill from the parsonage to Hermann Heights, picnic basket on Mama's lap. I stood for a moment quickly scanning the grounds of the park, trying to catch a glimpse of Rudi before I followed my parents to the picnic table. Such a beautiful park—on the top of a hill overlooking the town of New Ulm. At the edge of the clearing, far below, you could see a great length of the beautiful Minnesota River Valley. The river itself was hidden by oak, maple and cottonwood trees that also shaded the picnic tables scattered on the green, clean, well-kept lawn. The mighty statue of Hermann the Great, sword raised in triumph, dominated the entire park.

Under the trees, not far from the edge of the park I saw two beautiful, new pavilions. The one to my right had a big sign on it—BEER! A crowd of people were gathered around it. Mama would shudder at the sight, but what was New Ulm without beer?

You'd never know there was a war going on, I thought, as I climbed

33

out of the Ford car with Father and Mama and reached for the picnic basket Mama and I had packed.

There were so many students and parents and teachers milling about, laughing, slapping each other on the back, playing horse shoes and volley ball, cranking three gallon ice cream freezers and organizing three-legged, gunny sack races, that I could hardly tell one person from another. Did Rudi forget we were supposed to meet here, I wondered. Is he not coming after all? Is he too busy? Is something wrong at home? Worst possibility of all, did he fall in love with one of the beautiful dancers at the Prom and forget I existed?

"Hey, Em! Reverend Altenberg! Over here," I heard Victoria call and saw her standing up between her parents, waving frantically as if there were a fire.

Father and Mama and I joined the Beckers, and the Altenberg picnic basket was emptied on to the table already overflowing with food. There were pickled beets and pickled beans, pickled pig's feet and *Kartofel Salat*, *Kohlsalat* and *Bratwurst* and a crock of lemonade with a huge chunk of ice and lemon halves bobbing around.

I couldn't eat. I was sitting next to Victoria with my back to most of the picnickers, so I couldn't keep turning around searching for Rudi among them. But I could see new arrivals as they came into the park. So far, no Rudi.

We were almost finished with our ice cream, scooped in rich mounds and melting fast, when a tall, distinguished gentleman joined us at the table. The Mayor! Dr. Louis Fritsche, his gracious wife, and young son Ted, who would soon match his father in height.

I watched my father rise from the bench, shake the Mayor's hand and bow to Mrs. Fritsche in his courtly way. What elegance, those Turners, I thought, free-thinkers, community leaders, much trusted and respected by the whole town and all around the countryside. They all loved to talk to Father. He was trusted and respected and elegant, too. Pride brought a smile to my face, in spite of my secret worry.

"We were not treated courteously in Washington," Joseph Becker was saying to Father. "We were kept waiting on the Capitol steps all day—a disappointment after coming all that way. We'll have to write a petition and send it. If even a thousand people sign, it should have some effect, I really believe. That is one way that democracy can work. We must keep trying."

Mr. Becker added, "We have to make it abundantly clear that we are not against the draft—only sending draftees overseas. The young men should have a choice."

Mayor Fritsche nodded. "By all means."

"It's a fine idea," Father said. "But can petitions really make a difference at this stage?"

"I don't know," Mayor Fritsche answered. "But how else can our voice be heard?"

"Oh, this dreadful war," Rosa Becker added, shaking her head.

"By the way," Mama began, and I held my breath as I guessed what was coming. "Speaking of petitions, I have some material from the Women's Christian Temperance Union that I'm going to pass out after we've eaten. So many people here. Such a good chance."

I felt my cheeks grow warm with embarrassment. I knew the Beckers drank liquor—beer, wine. In moderation, of course. I looked down at my nearly full plate and was about to take a small bite of potato salad, when I felt Vicky poke me in the ribs.

"Come on, Em. Finish up. Let's go join the games. Excuse us, please," she announced as she gracefully lifted and then uncurled her legs from under the table. The maneuver looked easy to me because Vicky was wearing the bloomers she wore for gymnastics at the Turnverein. I had to bend and swing my legs, holding my skirt at the same time so my underwear wouldn't show.

"How about the relay race, Em?" Vicky asked. "Stefan is leading the one over there by the band stand."

"How am I going to run in a long skirt," I answered. "I think I'll just wander around for a while. Maybe play croquet."

"You don't mind if I don't go with?"

"Not at all," I answered quickly, this time not lying. This was my blessed chance to look for Rudi. If only they had agreed to meet in a certain place!

I strolled about the park, saying hello to friends, saying no, I didn't really care to join the games, trying to look natural, unanxious and as though I were enjoying myself. I heard the squeals and shouts of excitement and delight all around me. I saw flushed and happy faces. But no Rudi anywhere.

People were starting to gather up their picnic things. Girls straggled back to the tables, looking exhausted, fanning their faces with their hands. The boys wiped their perspiring necks with handkerchiefs. The picnic was drawing to a close.

Still, no Rudi.

I struggled to hold back tears that tightened my throat. This was worse than the prom. Was I going to feel left out of everything forever, just because of Rudi Meyerdorf?

"Hey, everybody, how about climbing Hermann before we go?" someone shouted above the murmur of the slowly thinning crowd.

I stopped in my tracks, turned around and looked at the growing cluster of classmates gathering at the foot of the statue. I lifted my face up to the helmeted bronze giant looming above me, spear in hand. I looked at the one hundred and ten iron stairs that circled around the base of the statue leading to the feet of Hermann the Great. I'd never liked Hermann, he looked so war-like; but people came from far and wide to climb to the top and look down at our city and our beautiful valley. Right now, the thought of climbing that far up with nothingness below me made a fierce chill slither up my spine like an icy snake. But I had to make this climb or I'd be left out of everything all my life.

I looked around at the excited, happy crowd still searching for the one face that meant the most to me and didn't see that face anywhere. I looked for my parents, checking to see if they were in a hurry to leave. They were still seated at the picnic table engrossed in politics and war talk and the rally, no doubt.

I turned back, facing Hermann the Great, "It's now, or never," I said to myself. "Maybe I can't dance, but I can climb!" I ran to join my friends, some already starting up the winding iron staircase.

At first, a feeling of elation almost overcame me as I felt myself in the midst of the crowd. The shoving of bodies in front and in back of me gave me a sense of safety and belonging. There were giggles and chuckles all around and I heard myself giggling, too. Even being close to Walter Ebers who was just ahead of me seemed good and right.

"There's nothing to it," Walter said over his shoulder. "I've done it hundreds of times. The view is great. Your turn next."

I lifted my skirt and took the first step. It was easy. The ten that followed were easy, too. Walter had been right. The second ten were even easier. And the third and fourth were not too bad, even though my heart started a frantic beating. It was on the fiftieth step, as the iron stairs were curving round the west side of the statue that I made my mistake. I looked down!

A blur of faces far below swam before my eyes. Cold sweat broke out all through me. My knees started to buckle. I gripped the railing with both hands and started to sink down onto the step. Far, far above me, I heard squeals of nervousness and delight from those who had already made it to the top. Was I going to faint?

Just as I felt myself slipping into nothingness, a warm hand covered my cold ones. "Just go on by," a voice said. "I'll stay with her."

Rudi! Rudi Meyerdorf's voice!

I couldn't look up or down. I couldn't let go of the railing. I clamped my fists more tightly than ever and leaned my head against the cold iron. Nausea lurched up from my stomach and into my mouth.

Rudi's familiar voice came to me from a distance, it seemed. "It's all right, Emma. Take your time. Everyone has gone on up. I'll stay with you until you feel better. Then, we'll go down together. Sorry I was late. Band practice."

I heard his voice, but could barely understand his words. They sounded far away.

Time stood still. It seemed like an eternity before I could lift my head just a little and look at Rudi. His face swam before my eyes. I still felt sick to my stomach. Didn't seem to care who was there or what happened to me. Not now. Not ever.

"Can you go down now, Emma? Are you ready?"

"I—I'm sick," I managed to say as bile started to gush from my stomach.

"Lean over the railing," Rudi said, and he handed me his handkerchief.

The little I had eaten came up, spewed out and fell to the ground below. There was a cluttering of steps as the climbers started to come down. I was faintly aware of Vicky passing by, offering to help, voices around me, faint, indistinguishable.

"I'll stay with her," someone said. Rudi?

"Could someone please go get her father?"

Did I say it or someone else? Did Rudi say it? I didn't care. Who was this picking me up in his arms? I felt too sick and weak to care about anything.

I knew I was being carried somewhere, but by whom? Finally, I was set down. I felt the solid ground under my feet and looked around at the swimming trees and lurching shadows. Edge of the park—must be. Strong arms holding my shoulders. A cool hand holding my forehead as I bent over and vomited again onto the ground. Handkerchief wiping my mouth. I began to feel better

And then, cool lips softly touched my cheeks. Whose?

I struggled to bring a face into focus. I saw it was Father. I turned into his arms and wept with relief.

"Thank you, young man," I heard Father say. I didn't dare look at the young man he was thanking. I knew who it was, but I was too ashamed to look at him. It was far, far too embarrassing. I hid my face in my father's shoulder as he carried me away from Rudi Meyerdorf.

CHAPTER SEVEN

July 25, 1917

I WAS DREAMING. In the dream, I was falling endlessly through the air, with no ground below me and no one to catch me. I was terrified. A chill of fear shot through my whole body and I woke up, trembling.

I sat straight up in bed and hugged myself to stop the shaking. I rubbed my forehead to erase the dream from my mind. It took me a while to shake off the dream and bring myself into the real, wide awake world. "This is my room. Here is my bed—my night table, lamp, treasure box . . ."

Treasure box! A feeling worse than fear gripped me—shame. The treasure box I'd longed to fill with some token from Rudi—Rudi—the climb—Rudi's hand touching mine—my heaving stomach—

I groaned and hid my face in my pillow to shut out the memory. But it did no good. The painful memory rolled on. I hadn't seen or heard from Rudi all the weeks since school let out. I told myself he was busy. But, really, I knew he must be avoiding me. He must be disgusted with my fear—my throwing up all over the place. But was it he who had kissed me on the cheek? And did Father see? He had not said a word.

Both Father and Mama reassured me that many people were afraid of heights. I was overheated, they'd said, excited, eaten too much. But it was no use. How could I ever live it down? If only I could see Rudi, talk to him, just for a little. But when? How?

And then, all of a sudden, I knew when! The thought jolted me into the day. I lifted my head from the pillow and glanced at the calendar on the wall, trying to reassure myself I wasn't still dreaming. No! I wasn't!

This was the day, circled in red, July 25th, 1917, the day of the big rally, with so many people hoping and praying that our petition would be heard in Washington and our boys would not have to fight friends and relations overseas.

There would be marching bands. Two of them! The first would be Hofmeister's Band of New Ulm. And in the front row would be Rudi Meyerdorf in his fine band uniform, captain's cap set neatly on his dark hair, shiny trumpet tucked under his arm. Maybe this very day, in Turner Park, at the rally after the parade, I would somehow manage to see Rudi, maybe even talk to him.

Victoria and I planned to meet and go to the parade together and then join Stefan Schroeder and Max and Bertha in Turner Park at the rally after the parade. We all offered to help pass out petitions before and after the speeches.

Hofmeister's band would have assembled in the park after the parade, seated themselves on the platform ready to play band music between the speeches. Somehow, just maybe, after the rally, I would find a way to get to Rudi and talk to him. I'd swallow my pride, somehow. It would be only natural to ask about his mother. His brother. And I had to believe he would forget what happened at the All-School Picnic.

Then, at that very moment, I heard a sound that plunged me into hopelessness again. The thrumping wasn't only my heart. It was raindrops drumming on the roof. Rain! Rain on the day of our rally and parade! This can't be!

"Oh, please, dear God, make it stop raining!"

I felt like getting down on my knees and pleading, which Father always said wasn't really a prayer, so instead, I slipped out of bed, dressed as quickly as I could and went downstairs to help Mama make sandwiches for out of town Methodists.

I greeted Mama as cheerfully as I could, "*Guten Morgan*, Mama. It's raining."

"*Ja*, sure." Mama said. "*Es macht's nichts aus.* It doesn't make any difference. I'm going ahead, getting ready, rain or no rain. New Ulm loves parades. A little rain isn't going to stop anybody in this town.

Cover the dining table with oil cloth, Emma. *Bitte*. Please. We need more space."

Father emerged from the Holy of Holies, pulling the curtains aside to look at the rain drumming against the windows, a sad, weary look on his face.

"Oh, Father," I said, feeling sorry for us both, even though our reasons for disappointment were not quite the same. "After all your planning!"

"We can hold the meeting in Turner Hall, if the rain continues. But people from the country and out of town. It's so hard for them when the roads get muddy. We'll have the rally, but not so many people will come. *Ach*, the things we can't foresee!"

"Here," Mama said, handing him *kuchen*, still warm from the oven. "Set these on the table to cool." Putting people to work was Mama's solution to problems, almost as good as coffee.

Father followed Mama's directions, absently looking out the window, again and again. When the table was filled with fragrant pastries, he went back into his study and shut the door. My heart ached for him, and for me, too. Mama's spirits bounced, like Victoria's. She kept on with her bustling, and I kept on helping her, looking out the window as Father had done and keeping my feelings to myself.

The morning dragged on and on. I peeled apples, rolled out pie crust, carried baked goods to church under my umbrella and prayed for the sun to come out, in spite of Father's not believing in using prayer that way.

By late morning, it did! Golden shafts of sunlight broke through the clouds and by mid-afternoon people from out of town began pouring in to the church. They soon filled the church basement, chattering with excitement about the change in weather and the promise of the day. They reached for coffee, liverwurst sandwiches and fresh pastries. Father came out of the Holy of Holies and joined his parishioners, greeting everyone, pitching in, helping me carry food from the parsonage to the church basement, serving coffee.

By late afternoon, as I carried the last two coffee cakes to the church, I heard the sound of cars grinding into town, horns honking. I stopped to listen and knew that it was the beginning of an exciting, momentous evening. I almost dropped the coffee cakes.

Just as the sun began to set, Victoria came tripping down into the church basement, looking beautiful beyond belief in a white dress with a huge red, white and blue bow nesting securely at the back of her head.

"Can you believe it, Em? All those people. Pater and all the rally planners will be so pleased! Let's go. We'll never get close to the parade if we don't go now."

"Run along, girls," Mama said from her station at the kitchen counter. "You've done enough. "You'll never see anything like it in all your born days. *Danke schön* for helping."

I couldn't believe my ears, Mama thanking me, sending me off to do what was so important to me. I dropped the spatula I was holding and hugged my mother. She would be staying behind, I suddenly realized, doing her kitchen duty as she always had. Was something changing about my feelings toward my mother? Was it me? Was it Mama? Whatever it was, I almost cried with gratitude and joy.

Father had been mingling with out-of-town Methodists all afternoon, greeting everyone, serving coffee, making liverwurst sandwiches. There was a twinkle in his eyes that I hadn't seen in a long time and when I looked at him, enjoying himself so much, all my insides twinkled with him.

"Meet us in Turner Park, girls," he said. "The program will be outside, now that the rain stopped. Good of you young people to pass out petitions."

"Glad to help, Father," I answered and hugged him warmly. "Oh, yes, I am!"

"Such enthusiasm. God bless you, *Liebchen*." He smiled, tucked his papers under his arm and waved goodbye to all the out-of-towners. "Enjoy the parade. Come to the rally. Sign the petition and God Bless!" he called before he left, looking as happy and hopeful, as I was beginning to feel.

Vicky grabbed my hand and practically dragged me out of the church basement, across the walk to the parsonage and up the stairs to my room. I pulled off my middie and changed to my best blue blouse as fast as I could. Vicky picked up my brush, set me in front of the mirror and started to brush the wisps of hair I'd messed up changing clothes.

"You're a moonlight blonde, Em," she said as she fastened a blue bow at the crown of my head with as many hair pins as she could find. "You should wear blue all the time. Come on. You look swell. Let's go."

With one last, swift glance in the mirror, I followed Victoria as she clattered down the stairs and out of the house with me trailing behind.

CHAPTER EIGHT

America the Beautiful

WE FLEW DOWN the street together, pushing through the huge crowds already gathering and found a place in front of Safferts Meat Market. A huge flag hung down almost to the sidewalk. We were breathless from hurrying, but managed to squeeze between two stout men and put our arms around the lamp post to keep from being jostled into the street.

Mama was right, for once, *Gott bei dankt!* I never hoped to see anything like this in my whole life again. I couldn't believe what was happening. Cars, cars and more cars kept grinding down the street—closed cars, open cars, Ford cars, mostly—hundreds and hundreds. There were horses and buggies, too, and even a few buckboards. This was a crowd beyond imagining.

Vicky recognized all of the different kinds of cars besides Fords. "Look," she said, grabbing my arm in excitement. "There's a Cadillac—a Studebaker—can you believe it—a Maxwell!"

"Mostly Ford cars, though," I answered, feeling as though I had to defend the people who couldn't afford such expensive autos. "Look at that buckboard with a whole family in it. Have you ever ridden one? I have. With Karl. Shakes your insides out."

Vicky was so enthralled with all the fine, new cars, she didn't seem to hear me.

"Der mus be tousants uff peoples," the stout man behind me said.

"*Ja,* und da parat hasn't effen shtartet," the other answered. "Dis rally iss going vay beyont expectinks!"

"*Hast du immer* so many peoples *gesehen*?" a woman said, awe and excitement in her voice.

"Nein! Dieser rally ist sehr gut geplannt, gel?" the tall, thin man beside me answered.

"Ja, ja!"

Victoria giggled and whispered in my ear, "New Ulm Deutsch, Emma, *ja?*"

I nodded, hoping the people next to us hadn't heard her.

The sun was still lingering in the evening sky when the sound of rolling drums announced that the parade had begun. A county dignitary led the parade. I recognized him, Louis Vogel, our county auditor. He carried a large flag, and marched with dignity, leading Hofmeister's Band of New Ulm, finest in all of the Midwest.

And there was Rudi, sure enough, in the front row. I waved and waved. I waved so hard my satin bow slipped off and I had to hold it in my sticky hand. Of course he didn't see me or hear me. He couldn't. He was looking straight ahead, back straight, head held high. My heart nearly burst with pride. My English pupil, my friend. My love?

Hofmeister's band was followed by another band. Then came the enlisted men followed by ordinary citizens, rally supporters, all of them were carrying flags and waving them. The crowd broke into cheers so loud you couldn't have heard a cannon if it had gone off in the street.

Without warning the joy inside me died. "Oh, Vicky!" I gasped and reached for Vicky's hand. "Look! Mr. Klemm! He's really enlisted!"

Vicky stopped her yelling and waving and clasped my fingers. "Yes, Emma," she answered suddenly sober. "He has. It's close to home, now, this war."

Vivid pictures filled my mind, taking me away from the excited crowd around me. We've been flooded with pictures in the newspapers, pictures of the horrors of war—the wounded, the sick and dying, the blind, men without legs or arms, battlefields with skeleton trees stripped of leaves, buildings in crumbled ruins, nothing recognizable anywhere.

Boys and men I knew were going off into that nightmare of a world. Golden-haired Mr. Klemm was one of them. Imagining Mr. Klemm as one of those maimed and suffering men, I forgot petitions and Rudi and the cheering crowd, the flag waving. Instead of being here on Minnesota Street, July 25th, waving and yelling myself hoarse, I was back on that spring day last April. I could just hear Mr. Klemm saying, "I am an American, and I want to do what is best for my country."

I just stood now, this day, happy shouting going on around me. I couldn't move. I couldn't possibly yell anymore.

Vicky's voice cut through my memory and brought me back to the here and now on Minnesota Street, July 25th, 1917. "Let's get to the park before the crowd," she said.

She hung onto my hand as we shoved and pushed and squeezed back away from Minnesota Street and hurried to Turner Park, where the rally was being held. Cars were parked for blocks on both sides of the streets, in front of Turner Hall, all around the park right next to the hall. The side walks were filled with people, walking fast to find a place under the trees where they could still see and hear the speakers and music. The park wasn't very big, really, but shady and well-groomed and could still hold lots and lots of people. It was already filled with people when we got there. They stretched from the platform, which was draped with red, white and blue bunting, all the way to the street behind. People, people everywhere, many I knew, many were strangers from out of town. They milled about talking, reading the white petitions that were being handed out, nodding to one another, shaking hands.

"*Gröss Gott.*"

"*Guten Abend.*"

There was a sea of people all around us, men in overalls, shirt sleeves rolled up and collars open. Some of the women were bare-headed, others wore hats and fanned themselves with Funeral Parlor fans. Some came in house dresses. But somehow, in all that crowd we found the faces we were looking for, Bertha and Max and Stefan's.

"Vicky, Emma! Did you ever—? What a crowd," Stefan said as he handed us some petitions and then took Vicky's arm.

"This is really something," Max agreed, excited. "We've got to write it up for the *Graphos*."

Bertha reached out and touched Max's arm, gently restraining him. "It's too political for a school paper. They wouldn't let us. And besides, school is more than a month away."

Max covered Bertha's hand with his own. "You're probably right. *Schade*, too bad. But take notes, Bertha. We might use it sometime. This is historic, you know."

I looked at the two couples, Max and Bertha, Vicky and Stephan. This must be what they mean when they say, "the fifth wheel in the wagon." If only Rudi and I—. I didn't finish the thought, but looked over at the band stand to see if the musicians had arrived at the park.

Just in time. The uniformed band members were working their way through the crowd, carrying their instruments and finding their seats on the platform. There was Rudi, in the front row. He didn't look out at the crowd trying to search me out, as I was hoping, but kept his eyes on his director.

Hofmeister stood before his band and lifted his baton. The musician's raised their shining instruments and sounded the first notes, the opening bars of "America the Beautiful." The program was about to begin. The crowd hushed.

After the introduction to America, Hofmeister turned to the hundreds and hundreds of people crowded below him and with a lift of his baton and a nod of his head, invited all the people to sing.

I saw Father standing in front, just below the platform, tall and stately, so close to Rudi, looking triumphant, a look I'd seldom seen on his face lately. It had been so grave for so long. I was sure everyone could hear his deep bass voice. ringing out above all the rest. Shivers of pride, in Father, in our country, mingled with happy tears as I sang along, loud as I could. At that moment I was even proud of being German-American, proud of the people of New Ulm.

After the music, the crowd quieted, and the flag was slowly raised. When it was fluttering grandly above us, Dr. Fritsche, tall, handsome, dignified, walked to the center of the platform and the crowd cheered. He placed his hand over his heart and began, "I pledge allegiance—"

We all followed him in one, great roaring voice.

After the Pledge of Allegiance, the band struck up the National Anthem and everybody sang again. "Oh beautiful for spacious—"

"Germans sure can sing," Max said when the anthem was over. "Even the high notes, they get. Listen, Bertha. It's starting."

Bertha, who came prepared with her stenographer's pad and pencil, started scratching and I looked at her scratches in wonder. Shorthand! How could she do it and how could she listen and scratch away at the same time.

I raised my head from Bertha's paper and watched Dr. Fritsche, so calm, so confident. He greeted the crowd in English and then began, "Today, only proper, peaceable and legal means would be discussed"— and ended in his clear, strong voice—"we hope and pray that this conflict may be solved before long and that our beloved land may revert to a state of peace which we all desire so much." Father's sentiments exactly.

Dr. Fritsche then turned to Major Pfaender, "Ladies and gentlemen, may I introduce our city attorney, who distinguished himself in the Mexican Border War and has long been connected with the military organization of this state. He will explain the purpose of this rally."

Major Pfaender began quietly. Bertha scratched furiously. Max beamed at her and then raised his head and beamed at Major Pfaender. Vicky laid her head on Stefan's shoulder.

"I must begin by urging you young men who have been drafted to obey the law. Congress has the right to call every able-bodied man into service of the country."

A roar of approval rose form the crowd.

"At the same time," he continued when the roar had quieted, "it is up to us who remain to use every honorable means in our power to bring about a constitutional amendment providing for a national referendum on the question of war."

Another roar of approval rose from the crowd. *"Ja! Ja!* Here! Here! Yeh! Yeh!"

"Whatever is done to protest this war, let it be done openly and orderly. Let it not be said that you are not loyal Americans—Let us continue in respect to the flag of which we are all so proud, so that there may be real truth in the beautiful words of our National Anthem,

In triumph shall wave,
O'er the land of the free
and the home of the brave.

A hush followed Major Pfaender's closing words as he walked sedately from the platform. I looked over at Rudi. His trumpet was ready. Hofmeister raised his baton and the strains of the Battle Hymn of the Republic rang out from the band, above the thundering applause. "Mine eyes have seen the glory—"

Rudi and the band played a patriotic air after each of the speeches, Captain Steinhauser, Mr. Retzlaff, Professor Wagner from Luther College who made his speech in German, and the Director of the College, Professor Ackermann. There was mention of freedom of speech and assembly, the right to petition, always mentioning the loyalty of the German-Americans in New Ulm and all over the state.

Excitement mounted. The cheering went on and on. The band responded. Major Pfaender read the petition:

Vowing our loyalty to this country and pledging in its defense the highest sacrifices to the extent of life itself if need be, and with full realization of the difficulties that beset a government in times of war, we respectfully petition the President and Congress of this nation not to transport or force across the ocean to the battlefields of Europe any men outside of the regular army, contrary to their desires, but that such matter be left to voluntary enlistments.

When he finished, another hush fell and at a motion from Hofmeister, Rudi stood up and raised his trumpet to his lips. The notes of taps sounded clear and pure in the quiet air, calling the audience to attention with his trumpet. Hofmeister raised his baton again and for the second time, the strains of "America, the Beautiful" floated across the crowd in the deepening summer night. The thousands of voices singing rose above the sound of the band.

I shivered with wonder. This was like church, much like church, I thought, only lots and lots more people and maybe even holier. I felt Vicky's arm around me, saw each of my friends, arms around one another, melded like a chain. We were all singing with tears in our eyes, even the boys.

When the last note faded away, the crowd started mingling again. None of us had time to pass out the petitions Max gathered for us. People reached for them now. The two couples moved among the crowd, petitions in hand, leaving me with a hug and a swift "goodbye." Blessedly for me, Father was still close to the bandstand just below Rudi's seat. He was shaking hands, keeping the ink bottles filled, passing out pens for people to sign the petitions.

Rudi closed his instrument case as I walked up. He saw me. He looked at me. He smiled, a dazzling smile that made my knees weak. He snapped his trumpet case shut, picked it up and walked right over to me. Looking right into my eyes with a look that seemed to say, "Forget about what happened at Hermann's Heights."

"How are you? How have you been, Emma?"

"I've been just fine." What could I do but lie?

"Well, *es freut mich*, I'm glad."

He put his trumpet case in his left and with his right hand, picked up my hand and kissed it. I thought I would surely die. With a brief smile and a nod, Rudy turned and walked away.

I didn't mind at all that my friends had left the park without me. I looked at Father in a daze. I didn't even mind if he saw Rudi kiss my hand.

But he seemed not to have noticed. He was busy closing the ink wells, picking up the pens and the last few petitions. When he finished, he took my arm, we said a few *"wiedersehens"* as we walked through the thinning crowd and left Turner Park.

I walked along beside my absent-minded, but exultant Father, floating on a cloud, the strains of "Oh, beautiful for spacious skies" still ringing in my ears. This is the most beautiful day of my life, I thought. Everything and everyone is beautiful—my father, my mother, too, my friends, all the wonderful people of New Ulm. All of America is beautiful! Both Father and I practically skipped home to the parsonage.

CHAPTER NINE

The Aftermath

"HARDLY TIME TO eat around here," Mama said, but there was no complaint in her voice. The telephone had rung off the hook all week and the stack of telegrams on the dining table grew larger each day. I watched the twinkle in Father's eyes grow brighter with each phone call. And the telegrams! So unusual. We'd only had a few in our wholes lives before this. Only when grandmother died. So much cheer in ten words!

"Congratulations. Rally resounding success. Pray petition will be granted."

"Rally inspiring. Hope for democracy. Hope for the world. Congratulations."

"Great rally. Thank you. Praise New Ulm for courage,"

It was Sunday morning. Father came down the stairs in his frock coat, Bible and hymnal tucked under his arm. He squared his shoulders and smiled broadly as he walked into the kitchen. My worries about his melancholy were fading each day. How much one rally could do, I thought, remembering how much it had meant to me—in more ways than one. I still felt Rudi's kiss on my hand.

Father said. "Now we go to church and thank the good Lord for all He has done for us and thank the congregation for its support. And today I preach on 'Greater Things Than These Shall We Do.'"

"We have food left from yesterday." Mama said, as she patted his shoulder. "Why not ask the congregation for coffee after the service. To celebrate."

"*Ja, ja!*" Father answered, kissing the top of Mama's head. "*Gut, gut.* I will. Now I must go. You come?"

"Right away, Father," I answered and Mama added. "I, too, as soon as Emmeline and I finish the dishes."

The service was wonderful. There was an air of hope and confidence all through the congregation that hadn't been there for months. Father's deep voice had a lilt and the people responded with brisk whiskings of their fans and every now and then a soft "Amen!"

After the service, most of the members gathered around the coffee pot and crock of lemonade in the church parlor, praising father for his sermon, Mama for her *kuchen*, praising the rally.

"What a wonderful country to be holding a rally like this. So many people. Wilson and Congress will surely heed our petition.

"It was a wonderful rally," one caller said. "Just wonderful. So dignified. So patriotic."

"And Pfaender—so clear. So smart. All of them. Wonderful. They said what we feel. Most of us with relatives still in the Old Country."

"That Mayor of yours, that Fritsche. So dignified. So smart. And the others. Vogel, Steinhauser, Reverend Ackermann. What they said is how we feel."

"What a country, America. Can you imagine this happening in a small town in Germany?"

On Monday morning Joseph and Rosa and Vicky Becker came over for breakfast as they often did. Dr. Becker was carrying a briefcase full of letters and telegrams and editorials that had been received by the leaders of the rally. He poured them all out on the kitchen table for us to read. It was exciting to see New Ulm's rally reported and praised in so many papers all over the countryside. Eight thousand people came, we read.

Only one newspaper account of the rally puzzled me. I read it out loud, feeling strange and a little fearful.

New Ulm, Brown County, where English is hardly ever spoken, is, figuratively speaking, up in arms against the United States government, and may secede from Minnesota and the Union and declare itself a "free city" of Germany. It would be too bad if we should lose New Ulm, for it is a pretty little city, manufactures a fine grade of beer and some mighty fine people live there.

"Now did you ever!" Mama chuckled. "How ridiculous!"

"One insolent report is not going to spoil our success," Rosa Becker added. "Any more of that good *apfel kuchen*, Anna?" She took the offending newspaper from me, folded it and put it back into her husband's brief case. Dr. Becker nodded and snapped the brief case shut.

"Nothing is going to dampen our spirits," Vicky said. She put her arm around me and we followed our mothers into the kitchen.

We should have taken that one report as a warning, like distant thunder rumblings before a storm, but we didn't. So it seemed as though the fury cracked down on us like the funnel of a cyclone hitting all at once. It happened about three weeks to the day after the rally.

I was helping Mama can tomatoes, when Father walked into the kitchen. I could tell, by the slump of his shoulders, that something was wrong. I remembered what Victoria said that day that hurt me so, "You worry too much about your father," so I didn't run to him, as I used to do. But my heart ached just the same.

"Mama, Emma—I think trouble is brewing. I don't want to worry you, but—" He plopped a stack of papers on the kitchen table and my eyes started to blur as I read:

> Is it any wonder that there are those who regret that the Sioux didn't do a better job of eliminating New Ulm fifty-five years ago?

Mama and I read, first from one paper, and then another. Words like traitors, traitorous mayor, yellow-bellies, sedition, leaped out at me. My father, Victoria's father, our beloved Mayor Fritsche, hard-working, God-fearing Onkel Grossbach, traitors? I couldn't believe my eyes.

I looked at Father, forgetting Victoria's words, and ran to him, threw my arms around him and buried my face in his shoulder.

I heard the crumpling of paper. Mama was having one of her fittys, that I called her indignant reactions to things she thought unjust. No tears for her. "What's the matter with those newspaper people," she fussed. "They don't know what they're talking about! How dare they pick on New Ulm!"

And with that she swished into the kitchen. I could hear the water run as she filled the coffee pot.

"Well, now," Father said, releasing me from his shoulder. "We mustn't take this too hard. There are lots of people in other parts of the state that are from Germany and understand how we feel. It may not be as bad as these papers make it sound." He gave me a pat on the shoulder and went into his study. I just stood there, too numb to move.

The telephone rattled and the door bell rang, both at the same time. Father answered the phone in his study and Mama flew out of the kitchen and went to the door. The moment she opened it I knew, for once, my father was wrong. Things were worse than those papers made it sound.

Victoria and Rosa Becker were standing at the door, Rosa clutching a folded newspaper in her arms. They both just stood there motionless, not saying a word, but looking as if they had been wrung through the ringer of a washing machine.

"*Ach*, Rosa, come in, come in," Mama said. "*Was ist los?* What's the matter?"

At the sound of Mama's voice, Rosa stirred, stepped into the house and collapsed in Mama's arms. Victoria flew to me and still without saying anything, the four of us just stood there, hanging on to each other.

"I'm sorry, so sorry, but I didn't know where I'd rather come at a time like this," Frau Becker said, when she'd recovered a little.

"What is it, Rosa?" Mama asked as she drew her down on the couch beside her. Victoria looked at me, smiled weakly as I pulled her into our easy chair and sat down on the floor at her feet and patted her knee.

After a moment, Rosa Becker regained some of her poise and opened the newspaper she had been carrying folded against her. "Have you seen this?" she asked.

Huge headlines stared at us from the front page of the *Minneapolis Journal*:

MAYOR OF NEW ULM ACCUSED OF TREASON!

Mama and I read the rest of the report, word for word. The rally had been a protest of the draft, the article said, and the mayor and organizers were under suspicion for anti-American, pro-German sentiment and under investigation by the Minnesota Department for Public Safety. New Ulm, a strongly German enclave in southern Minnesota, is a hot-bed of seditious and subversive activity.

Mama didn't sputter. She just sat there beside Rosa and held her hand. Frau Becker took a deep, quavering breath and then, went on. "There's more—there's even more. Someone sent from the Safety Commission broke into the Fritsche's house and searched it from top to bottom for hoarded sugar and flour. He turned the house upside down and all he found was a small box of stale cake flour. Mrs. Fritsche was alone except for her youngest son, Ted. He—he must have been terribly frightened. How could an eleven-year-old do any-thing to protect his mother!"

Young Ted. I remembered his grave face at the picnic. And gracious Mrs. Fritsche, our very own mayor's wife. How could this be happen-ing to them—to people we knew, admired and cared so much about? I looked up at Victoria and saw a look on her face much like the one I saw the day we had our first—and last, quarrel. Tears were filling her eyes.

Rosa took another deep breath and went on, "Mrs. Fritsche became hysterical—I don't blame her—I would have, too—and she called Dr. Fritsche who called our police and they threw the man out—out of their house—their private home! Joseph is indignant—furious. But all I feel is—is fear!"

Father must have heard the last of Rosa's story just as he came out of his study. His sad and brooding look had darkened into a scowl.

"That telephone call. It was Dr. Strickler. Mayor Fritsche has been suspended from office. Albert Pfaender, too."

There was a small quick, gasp. "Suspended?" Frau Becker's whispered.

Father nodded. "Just suspended. Not removed from office. They couldn't do that."

"How can they do this?" Mama spit out.

Father answered, "It's the Commission for Public Safety, appointed by the governor to root out subversion and disloyalty." His voice was low. "We seem like a danger, somehow. Like we are a contagious disease."

"Because we're German?"

"Because we're German—German-American."

We sat in silence for an eternity, it seemed. The only sound in the room was the steady, faithful ticking of the clock, Grossmutter Altenberg's hand-carved clock that had come all the way from Germany.

It was as though we were sitting in a fog that covered us all—even Mama, who sat with her plump arm around elegant Frau Becker and didn't move a muscle. We were all paralyzed, bewildered—silenced.

What had silenced us so quickly? What was happening to us? What more was to come? Rosa Becker had used the word—fear. I felt it course through me like an icy river. I groped for something safe, reached out, found Victoria's hand and held on to it tightly.

CHAPTER TEN

Us Girls

"WHAT'S GOING TO happen to us, Reverend Altenberg?" Vicky asked Father.

The scowl on Father's face softened into a gentler look as he smiled at Victoria. "I don't know what is going to happen to us, but we mustn't lose our courage. We have done nothing wrong—nothing unconstitutional. We must have faith. This is America, after all. Here we have freedom of speech and assembly."

Mama stood up. "Coffee, everyone? We all need a good hot cup, I bet!"

Rosa Becker stood up, too, clasped her small hands together and managed a little smile. "You always know what we need, Anna Altenberg," she said, and followed Mama into the kitchen. Father excused himself and disappeared into his study.

As soon as the grown-ups had left the room, Vicky plopped herself down on the floor beside me and we hugged each other silently for a long time. This was the first time we had been alone together since the day of the rally—just us girls.

"Who'd ever think this was going to happen," Vicky said as she released me and wiped away the tears. "After that great rally. I wonder what it will be like at school after this. What will everybody think now?"

"I don't know. I sure hope we don't go on arguing all the time. It's awful. I hate it."

"Well, I know what Stefan will think. And Max and Bertha. But Walter and those that were so for this war. Will they be lumped in with all the rest of New Ulm? And what about Rudi, Em? Where will he stand? You must know. You can't tell me anymore that something isn't going on between you two. I saw him carry you down from Hermann at the All-School Picnic. He wouldn't even let me help you. Come on now, confess! Something's going on, isn't there?

"Oh, Vicky, I'm sorry. But I just can't talk about it. Especially now after I got so scared and threw up all over the place."

"He sure looked like he cared about you, picking you up in his arms like that. How come you've lied to me?"

"I haven't lied to you really, about Rudi and me. I've been so upset and confused. I mean, I don't know if there's anything going on between us or not, but I just couldn't talk about it. Afraid if I talked about it, it might spoil something."

Victoria wrapped her arms around herself shivering with excitement. "So there is something! I knew it! But why couldn't you tell me? I'm your best friend, remember?

How could I tell her the truth?—that I was, well, jealous, I guess, and didn't trust her when it came to boys. "I don't know, really," I made myself say. "You have so many boy friends and all. You know all about things like that. I'd be embarrassed."

"Oh, I don't know all about it, Em. I mean, Rosa and I have talked, but I still don't know everything. I've been alone with boys a lot, and Stephan Schroeder kissed me eighty-three times one night, but I still don't know everything. You know?"

"You mean, you counted?"

"Well, it wasn't very interesting, really, and I was curious about just how long he would keep it up. But how about you and Rudi, Em? Have you ever been alone with him?"

"Well, no. I mean, yes—in a way. We were alone in the music room at school and we talked a lot after our lessons—about our families. Things like that."

"But that doesn't give you much chance to—well, you know—"

"Oh, Vicky, it's been terrible—but wonderful, too. I saw him after the rally. After you and Stefan left. And—he kissed my hand."

"Your hand, Emma? That's absolutely *de rigueur*! Like the courts of Europe. But didn't you want him to—you know—take you in his arms—or anything?"

"Oh, Vicky, it's so hard to talk about. You're so much more worldly-wise than I am. You've learned so much about manners and things like that from your mother. And mine is—well, all for the kitchen and our house and the church and prohibition."

"Em! Your Mama is warm and funny and spunky, don't you think?"

"*Ja*, true. But she doesn't know much about, well, life. I've never even been to a picture show, like you have. You go all the time and you get to dance with the boys at Turner Hall."

"Oh, go on with you, Em. You're so much more grown-up than I am. Rosa says so. She says you are old for your age, wise beyond your years. Go on, tell me about you and Rudi. I won't laugh at you, believe me, and I won't tell a soul, I promise."

I searched Victoria's face. It was such a relief, talking to her. I had to trust her. Who else was there?

"Well, there isn't much more to tell—except—"

"*Ja*? Go on, Emma, except what?" Victoria prodded, her eyes shinning.

"Well, there's one thing more, but I'm not sure I remember it very well, feeling so sick and everything. But I think, Vicky, that over at the edge of the woods, before Father came, I think he kissed me—on the cheek."

Vicky listened to each word as if I had just disclosed the greatest secret in the world.

"Oh, Emma, that's sweet. But didn't you want him to, you know—take you in his arms and really kiss you?"

"Then, Vicky? All vomity and everything?

"Well, not then, maybe, but ever? I mean, really, Emma. Sweet sixteen and never been kissed? Are you going to wait any longer?"

All of a sudden, I crumpled and started to cry. "I don't know what's happening to me lately. There's a war going on and there's all that's happening in our town—Mr. Klemm and the Fritsches—and—and—I've been so cross, so teary—so mixed up!"

"You mean about Rudi? About your feelings about a Catholic boy? One from Goosetown? Land's sakes, I wouldn't want to be in your shoes. I mean, Pater and Rosa don't worry about kissing or dancing and playing cards or things like that, but they probably wouldn't like it too much if I fell in love with a Catholic. I think—"

"You think what, Vicky? What's wrong with Catholics, anyway? We're all people and the Gags are Catholic, I think, and look how talented Wanda is. And her sisters. Artistic like you wouldn't believe."

"I don't know exactly. We don't think they're dirty or mean or anything like that, but I think it has something to do with the Pope, believing in everything he says. But then, you believe in everything your father says, don't you? Is that because you're Methodist, or because you're German?"

At the mention of my father, the same irritation I felt before, started to rise up again, but it didn't rise very far. This time, I really needed Vicky's help. I pleaded, "I don't know what's German and what's Turner or Methodist or anything anymore. Father thinks of German as Bach and Beethoven and poets like Goethe and Schiller and the woods in his homeland."

Vicky nodded with understanding, saying, "And Pater thinks what's German are philosophers like Kant that sit around and think and discuss all the time."

I continued, "And Mama thinks of German food like sauerkraut and keeping clean and orderly and having babies. She's always been sad that she's had only me."

Vicky was suddenly sober. "My cousins in the East want to forget they're German, especially the kind that wear lederhosen and funny little hats. I don't know what it means, really, to be German, German-American. Certainly we don't all want to build guns and submarines and want to rule the world. I'm like you, Em. I don't know what I believe, these days. How about Methodists, Emma. What do they believe in?"

"Well—I guess—we believe in God the Father Almighty and in Jesus Christ his only son, our Lord who taught love and peace and good-will among men. At least that's what my father thinks. And I guess most Germans believe the father is the head of the household and should be obeyed. But I always thought my parents were different, somehow."

"So why don't you talk to them, then? I can almost always talk to Pater and Rosa. They have definite opinions, that's for certain, but they tell me I have to exercise my mind and figure things out for myself. Pater says your father is more of a free thinker than he knows. So why don't you talk to him? Ask him what's wrong with Catholics. Are you afraid to get in an argument with him? He's not God Almighty. Is he?"

That shaky thought stopped me cold. And there was that strange question again. I couldn't think of anything to say, so I said nothing, remembering one of Mama's favorite proverbs, "Be silent, or say something better than silence."

Mama and Frau Becker came out of the kitchen, both smiling a little weakly, but smiling, anyway. Did they ever talk about things, personal things, like Vicky and me? Something had eased their fears. Mama's coffee, maybe.

When the *wiedersehens* had been said and the Beckers left, Mama went back into the kitchen. I still sat on the floor, thinking, thinking, going over all that had happened during this long, weary morning. In my mind, I heard Victoria's last words, again, "He's not God Almighty, is he?"

Is he? In my mind, I knew he was not. Another part of me was not so sure I hadn't got the two confused. What was happening to me? There's war in our town—in our state, our country—in the world. And there certainly is a war inside me. Will it never end? Will peace in all these places ever come again? Especially the one inside me?

CHAPTER ELEVEN

The Color Yellow

IT WAS SATURDAY, a most beautiful early autumn morning, warm and balmy. School had started and the routine of schedules and homework and getting back to school to see everybody helped a little to lighten the cloud of suspicion that was hovering over every-thing. I woke to the sound of Mama in the kitchen, probably canning apple sauce. Father was outside, raking leaves. The swish of the rake beneath my window was like a call for me to get up.

"It's too beautiful to stay inside," Father said when I joined him to pick up a pile of leaves. "Not many more warm ones left. Tell Mama. We go to the country today, *nicht wahr?* We go calling. We need to get out in the country. We go see Oma at the farm. She is failing daily."

On the way to the Grossbach's this day, Father yelled above the grinding rattle of the car. "I'm worried about Dietrich, too. Karl passed his eighteenth birthday and is supposed to register for the draft. He says he definitely won't let Karl go to war."

"What can he do?" Mama shouted back.

"*Ich weiss nicht.* I don't know. He's talking about having him hide out at his brother's cabin in the Northwoods. I just wish he wouldn't go around town talking like that. It's not good for him. Or for Karl. The walls have ears."

Karl, drafted! I forgot that he was old enough. Gentle Karl, hiding away in the woods. Or would he be one of those that suffered and bled in the trenches of Europe. The war was getting much too close to home.

We knew, the moment we drove up to the Grossbach mailbox, that something was dreadfully wrong. Their mailbox, sticking up above the weeds by the lane that led to the farm house, was painted a bright, ugly yellow!

There was a big, black car in the yard, beside the hayrick. Not a Ford car like ours, but a big, black Studebaker. There was no one in sight, but the sound of angry voices came from behind the house, near the barn.

We scrambled out of the car, Father running toward the voices and Mama and I flying into the house as fast as we could, without even knocking.

Oma was propped up in bed, head bowed, one arm around each of the little boys, whose faces were buried in her shoulders. Tante Grossbach and Amelia were at the window looking out, backs rigid. They were so intent they must not have heard us come in, but when Mama said *"Ach, vas!"* Tante turned around, saw Mama, and flew into her arms. Everyone was flying into Mama's arms these days, it seemed. Amelia stayed glued to the window.

Tante pressed her fist into her mouth, like she was trying to keep from screaming. Oma was motionless, frozen in her bed, her small grandsons curled up against her. Amelia motioned to me to come to the window and I kneeled down beside her.

Outside, in front of the barn were four men, besides Onkel Dietrich and Father. A huge American flag stretched out between two of them. They held it against the side of the barn. Another man struggled with Onkel, whose arms he held tightly. It looked like he was trying to tie them with a rope.

The fourth man confronted Father. I couldn't believe what I was seeing! Father in a fight? Father, the pacifist? But no, Father was not fighting. He was reaching out, trying to hold the man with one hand, while he tried to reach Onkel with the other. He was not winning the struggle.

"Here, here," Father said, *"Was ist los?* What's the matter?"

"Stay out of this, Reverend, if you know what's good for you. It's none of your business," one of the flag men shouted.

"*Ja*, Christian, *ja*, go home!" Dietrich gasped. "It's not your fight! It's mine!"

"*Nein*, Dietrich, I'll not leave until these men let you go! I'll report this to the authorities!"

All four men laughed, ugly laughs. "What authorities? You don't think you Krauts in New Ulm have any authority! Now, prove you're not a traitor, Mister Herr Gross-ass! Get down on your knees! Kiss the flag, you yellow-bellied son of a bitch!"

"Kiss the flag! Kiss the flag!" All four men yelled. You could have heard them in the next county.

Inside Oma's bedroom, Mama held on to Tante to keep her from running out in the yard. Amelia ran to Oma and the boys. I stayed at the window, watching in horror.

The man that grabbed Father released him and ran to Dietrich, Father still hanging on to him, trying to restrain him. If only he would punch him and knock him out! But then, two against four?

"Kiss the flag! Kiss the flag, coward," they kept shouting and pushed Onkel toward the barn, forcing him to his knees and shoving his face against the flag.

"Let's hear the kiss, Kraut!"

"Gentlemen! Men! Whoever you are!" I heard Father's loudest, deepest pulpit voice boom out. "That's enough. Four against one. What kind of brave men are you?"

It was not a fist punch, but a punch, just the same. The men let Onkel go and he slowly stood up and leaned against the barn, turning his face away from everyone. The men brushed their clothes and folded the flag.

"Since you're a reverend—well, we got what we came for," one of them said to Father.

"Almost," said another. "Where is that son of his, that yellow-bellied draft dodger? He'd better show up or next time it will be worse—for all of you!"

With that, they walked away. You could hear the roar of their big, black car growling its way out of the farmyard until it faded in the distance. I watched Father put his arm around Onkel Dietrich's shoulder.

I turned from the window where I'd been kneeling. I couldn't witness one more moment of Onkel's humiliation. I didn't feel like crying. What I had seen was too deep, too shocking and painful for tears. I walked into the bedroom in a trance. Tante and Mama sat on the bed, holding the boys, stroking Oma's hands. Her old eyes shifted from one boy to the other in frightened bewilderment. The ugly words with the flag had all been in English, so Oma could not have understood them. But there was no mistaking the actions and the fierce anger in the voices.

It was at that moment I realized that Karl was not here—had not been here the whole time. Why had I not realized it before? Karl gone! Where was he?

Onkel and Father were quiet when they returned. Not one word was said about the happening. Not one word about Karl. Even though I was worried to death about my dear friend, I thought it best not to ask questions now.

Oma asked Father to say a prayer, which he did—for peace, for strength. When he rose from his knees, we hugged one another, still in silence. And then we left. On the way home, the silence in the Ford car was heavy—and deep.

CHAPTER TWELVE

Tears and Laughter

"WHERE'S KARL?" VICTORIA whispered to me as we bent over the sink in the Girl's Room Monday morning. There were several other girls near us washing their hands. "I don't know," I whispered back. I was grateful Father had kept the secret to himself, if he himself knew. I didn't have to tell what I didn't know, he'd said.

Amelia had come back to school looking pale and drawn, but acting as though nothing was wrong.

"You all right?" I asked in a whisper when we met in the hall between classes. "How is Tante—Oma—your little brothers?" I couldn't bring myself to ask about Onkel—or Karl.

"We're all right. Doing fine," she answered with a small, weak smile. She squeezed my hand, and with a softly breathed, *"Danke,"* walked on to her next class.

A chill of fear curled around inside me as I tried to picture Karl, hiding away somewhere in the cold forbidding North Woods. I remembered the day last summer when he asked me to walk with him into the warm woods behind the farm. Sadness washed over me filled with the regret that I had not gone with him. Would I ever see him again, I wondered?

"Where's Karl?" By the end of the week that question hung in the air over the whole school. Bertha and some of the girls from Karl's class walked by Amelia and me as we talked to each other in low voices. Bertha gave us each a reassuring touch on our shoulders and then walked on. No one stopped to question us. It was as if everyone heard about the nightmare at the Grossbach's and knew that Karl had disappeared, but no one seemed to want to talk about it.

Erika was standing in front of the mirror, peering closely at her reflection. "Has anybody tried drinking sage tea for their complexion?" she asked to the room in general, with a small, forced laugh.

"Oh, *ja*, but it's not as good as Wyeth's Sage and Sulphur Compound," Anneke answered, touching her cheeks. "Can't you tell the difference in mine? Milky white and soft as dew?" She giggled nervously.

"I need to lose weight," Bernice said as she pulled up her skirt, showing her legs above her high-buttoned shoes. "Skirts are getting shorter. Our legs will show. What do you think?" And she giggled, too, looking at Amelia as though she were trying to cheer her up about something that hadn't even been mentioned.

"I like it," Victoria said. "Women can't wear long skirts forever. They're doing men's jobs now with the soldiers off to the war. And anyway, I like it. Look at our legs—they're pretty. Maybe by the time the war is over, they'll be up to here!" She lifted her skirt up to just under her knees where the bloomers began to show.

"I'd be ashamed to show my knees, they're so ugly. The boys would call me 'knobby-knees' for sure," Bernice said with a nervous titter.

The bell rang and the girls picked up their books started to leave the Girls Room, several of them patting Amelia on the shoulder as they left.

"It's not the same, is it, Em?" Victoria said to me as we walked down the hall. "We talk about the same things, but the fun's gone. We're not as easy with each other."

"I guess everybody is afraid to say too much—or ask too much. It might hurt someone's feelings or start an argument—or give somebody away. Mama always says, "Keep silent unless you can think of something better than silence."

"That's a funny thing for your mother to say, Em. She blurts right out what she thinks. She doesn't seem to be afraid of anybody. Well, clothes and boys are probably better than silence any old day, don't you think?"

I didn't say anything. I didn't feel like laughing these days. My heart was too heavy.

Laughter greeted me when I walked into the library Wednesday morning before classes began for the *Graphos* staff meeting, the same kind of nervous laughter.

"Better to have loved them all, than never to have loved at all!" Katrin was saying about our class Romeo. "I think we should put that in our paper this week, in the gossip column. That's rich!"

"*Du bist ein* hopeless case!" Raymond chuckled at Katrin.

"*Warum hast du nichts gelerhnt?* Why have you learned nothing? That's what Herr Schmidt always says to us. We could put that in," Bertha said with a grin.

"Should we put these things in the paper? Jokes about New Ulm German?" Katrin asked, a frown on her face. "Some people are sensitive."

I wasn't surprised that Walter picked up on that, "When are we going to stop thinking of ourselves as German!" It wasn't a question. It was a statement.

Then, looking all around the table, he went on, "We're Americans. Some of us are already overseas fighting for our country. Mr. Klemm, the best teacher most of us ever had has been shipped out, to France—or Belgium, or some trench over there. Some of us—" and he gave Amelia a quick glance before he continued, "Some of us are still resisting this war!"

I looked over at Amelia who sat with her hands in her lap, trying to keep her head up, but looking down often at her fingers and clutching them together. I wanted to go to her and put my arm around her, but I didn't dare. Everybody would look at her if I did, and we'd have to talk about Karl—and no one seemed to want to.

It was like at a funeral, when no one knew what to say, so didn't say anything, just nodded politely.

"Well," Katrin Elsworth began again, "I think we should leave some of this for the school annual. Maybe by then, the war—" She stopped. There was silence in the room.

All of a sudden, Max stood up and banged his fist on the table. "This is ridiculous. What are we, anyway? Cowards? This is a free country!

Freedom of speech—freedom of the press! We all know that the state has suspended the most popular mayor this town has ever had. We all know what the governor said about New Ulm! Can't we talk about these things without getting all hot under the collar? Just because we're High School students, can't we have editorials in our paper and express our opinions? We all know about the shameful Grossbach incident, don't we—?"

He looked over at Amelia, and then—at me!

My heart pounded. Was I supposed to say something?

It was our faculty advisor who saved me. Mr. Klingman walked in before a single thought came to me. Had he been asked to come? Had he been listening outside the door, eavesdropping? Of course, I tried to reason, it was his right, his responsibility.

He walked into the room, and slowly shut the door, slowly sat down.

"Think about it, people," he said. "There is a time to speak out, and a time to be silent. We are at war with Germany. We are a German-American community. Already with a reputation. You don't want to make matters worse? Do you?"

He cleared his throat, stared hard at us, and in a low, deep voice went on. "You may not realize it, people, but we have heard on good authority that the entire community may be interned! The entire city of New Ulm—interned!"

Max Brauer stood there speechless, motionless; and then slowly, carefully, sat down. No one stirred. No one spoke for a long time.

It was Walter Ebers who finally asked, almost in a whisper, "All of us? All of New Ulm? Even those who supported the war from the beginning?"

Mr. Klingman nodded, solemnly.

Walter ran his fingers through his hair, rubbing his head like he was trying to rub in an idea. "Who said, anyway? Why? Because we're German? I'm not German! I was born here. Would they lock up my parents and not me? Was it because of the rally? I didn't even go!"

"Not so fast, Walter. Internment. It's a rumor. Some attorney in the Cities wrote that all those New Ulmites had better watch out or they'd find themselves out on the prairie behind barbed wire. It was in the city paper. But there's lot of anger out there toward us."

Mr. Klingman had nothing more to say. Nor did Walter. No more questions from anybody. We just sat there. Anneke Hilfer finally broke the silence. "Well, we can always write about school activities—upcoming events, basketball scores—things like that."

"Or jokes," someone else said. But nobody laughed.

After school, I walked home slowly, hugging my books close to me, thinking, thinking. What did it mean to be interned? A whole town? A town filled with people who had left Germany because they didn't like many things there and thought it would be better, freer, here.

I looked around me at the neat, red brick houses, with fresh white painted porches, the graceful trees on the hill that hid the hospital where I was born. I looked to my right at the American flag waving on top of our beautiful United States Post Office and I remembered Major Pfaender's words at the rally, "Let us continue in respect for the flag of which we are all so proud." All this—interned? Shut in with police all around—or a stockade built surrounding us, closing us up from the rest of the world. How could they do that to us? Who would do it?

"Hey, Em!" the familiar voice called to me. "Wait up!"

Victoria Becker. I stopped and looked back at my friend. I was so glad to see her, running to catch up with me, waving wildly, her skirt flip-flapping as she ran. How easily and quickly she could make me forget the war and my father's depression and Karl and Rudi, even! Just walking beside her was a comfort, these days, so different from a few weeks ago.

"Good news," she bubbled. Fritsche and Vogel and Pfaender offered to resign to make it easier on New Ulm, so things aren't as bad as they could be. And anyway, Em, I've been thinking. Why don't you join something fun at school—like the Pep Club? Join the Daughters of Thespis and be in a play. We can't do the German plays anymore, they're not allowed, but we're doing 'Arms and the Man' by George Bernard Shaw. You'd like it, it's really swell. Take your mind off the war."

"Vicky! Don't tell me we can't have the German plays anymore. They made so much money last year. They're so popular! How come? Who said?"

"Well, who knows? The school board, I think. Somebody. They think we're all pro-German here. So they have to prove we're not. Nobody asked us students. We can't have German books in the library anymore, either. Well, anyway, what's done is done."

"What's going on with you, anyway, Em?" she rattled on, changing the subject quickly. "Besides the ghastly Grossbach thing. How about you and Rudi? You doing English with him this year yet?"

"No, Vicky. He hasn't asked me. He's different this year. Like everything else. I guess I have to face it. That's over. Whatever there was between Rudi and me."

"You're going to give up that easy? Why? If it were me and Rudi Meyerdorf didn't ask me about English lessons this fall, I'd ask him!"

"Oh, Vicky! I couldn't. How could I? I mean—a girl, asking a boy?"

"Why not, anyway? It's not like a date or anything. You have to teach him good and proper English, you know. It's your patriotic duty!" And with that she started to laugh and I couldn't help but burst out giggling, too. It felt so good.

After that, everything we said was funny. Especially, when she told me the pep yell Aimee Schmidt tried to get the girls to learn:

Hippety, chippety, hop-bop-boom
Whoopety, whoppety, zip, flip, zoom!
Kerslam, kerbif, hip-hip-hey.
New Ulm High School, Rah, Rah, Hooray!

"She said her cousin sent it to her from her college," Victoria sputtered between giggles that were keeping us from walking straight.

"Can't you just see Aimee bouncing up and down in her middie and bloomers, her bosom flopping?"

Vicky bent over, doubled up with laughter and her laughter was so contagious, I started laughing, too, just a little at first. And then, for no reason, it seemed, harder and harder. Pretty soon, we were laughing at each other laughing. Everything seemed so silly.

Then, I straightened up. The laughter inside me was gone. The tears that came from laughing so hard stopped. I clutched my books close to me again. They hid the place where my bosoms were supposed to be—the bosoms that didn't seem to ever get there. Rudi would see me at basketball games this winter. What would he think if he saw me in bloomers?

"Oh, Vicky. I—I look so awful in middies and bloomers. I'm so short! I—I can't be in the Pep Club. I just can't."

Victoria suddenly stopped giggling, too. She looked at me and her voice, once again, dropped into the soft, comforting sound that I welcomed this day.

"Emma, it doesn't matter. Really, it doesn't. I just thought it might help—being in the Pep Club—anything like that. It's helped me get over some things."

"Like what, Vicky?" I asked, "You never seem to have to get over anything."

"That's all you know about it, Emma Altenberg. You think I don't know your father or mother. Well, you don't really know mine—or me, for that matter."

"Vicky!"

"*Ja*, I know. We put on this stiff upper lip. And hide a lot with laughing. Pater and Rosa are as worried as your Father. And hurt. Anyway, it doesn't hurt to laugh, even when you're sad, does it?"

"I—guess not, Vicky—I guess it's—" I couldn't finish. Tears and laughter, I thought. Laughter and tears. So close, so close.

Victoria looked at me suddenly very sober. There was not a trace of a smile on her beautiful face. "Some town leaders are talking about changing the name of our street. They want us to call it Liberty Street instead of German Street."

"Oh, Vicky! That seems so sad. Why? Why is this all happening?"

"I guess it's a little thing, really," she answered. "But it's like anything German is so awful now. It's like we are supposed to forget our heritage. You understand?"

"*Ja*, Vicky," I answered. A bit of Mama's defiance rose up in me just then, and I answered in the German language, "*Ich verstehe*. I understand. For a while part of me wanted to drop the hyphen in German-American. Now, with all this hatred and suspicion, I want to put it back in."

Victoria hugged me, books and all, turned, and slowly walked toward her house. I told myself it was the same house, on the same street, with a new name; but still, her home. Why was just changing a name so strange and sad? It was sad for Vicky, too. Bouncy Vicky. Was she changing, too?

I took a deep breath, and then turned toward my own home.

CHAPTER THIRTEEN

The Lesson

I MADE UP my mind on the way home. No pretense of patriotism on earth could make me start talking to Rudi first. He'd have to be the one to begin. He'd been polite this fall, but so far there had been no mention of continuing the English lessons that had brought us so close last spring—or so I had thought. In spite of the smile and the courtly kiss on my hand after the rally, his feelings for me had changed, I was sure. He no longer cared about me. It was breaking my heart, but what could I really do about it? I felt helpless—about Rudi—about the war—about everything.

When I came into the house, the door to Father's study was open. He sat in his swivel chair, his back to the door. I could tell by the droop of his shoulders that one more dreadful thing had happened.

Father turned his chair around when he heard me. He held a stack of newspapers on his knees. He beckoned to me and held out the papers to me.

"Here," he said. "Joseph Becker brought these to me. He has been saving them from all around the country. You must read them. You want to be a writer some day. A woman journalist. I hope you never have to write this sort of thing."

I read the first headline. Ottumwa, Iowa:

SPEAKING GERMAN FORBIDDEN.

In smaller print were instructions to the citizens that they must not speak German, even on the telephone, or they would be prosecuted.

"Oh, Father! Will this happen here?" I dropped to the floor and pressed my face against his knees.

"I pray the Good Lord it will not. All the old people in my church know so little English. I have to preach to them in German or they will not be able to hear the Word."

The next headline:

ALL GERMAN BOOKS GATHERED AND BURNED.

I could read no further. Father's head was bowed and he rubbed his forehead with his long fingers, as though he were trying to ease the pain that must be there.

I let the papers slide to my feet and scatter.

"We must continue to have faith, *meine Tochter*, my daughter," he went on. "But *ach!* How my heart aches. All those beautiful books. Burned! The poets, the story tellers, Goethe, Schiller, Heinrich Heine—the philosophers, the scientists, the men who wrote against German nationalism and militarism—all burned! *Ich kann nicht verstehe.* I cannot understand."

He put his hand on my head and patted it as we both sat stunned and silent.

"That Red Cross lady," Mama sputtered as she came in the front door and closed it with a thump. "Teaching us to knit, making us knit so and so many socks and scarves in a week. She doesn't like us, I bet. Just because we're German. You'd think we had some sort of contagious disease, for sure. We've been down at the armory all afternoon, knitting. And I hate knitting. But if it helps those poor boys overseas—."

It was at that moment Mama noticed Father and me sitting as though we were in a trance, newspapers scattered around our feet. She put down her knitting bag and picked up one of the papers and started to read, "*Ach, mein Gott in Himmel*," she said, indignation pouring out of her round body. "What is the world coming to?"

We sat in silence until Mama finally said, "I guess I'd better get supper."

The very next day, Rudi waited after Glee Club practice until I gathered my music together. I had almost got used to his not noticing me, so I hadn't even looked over at him when we finished practice. His voice startled me. I caught my breath when I looked up and saw him.

"Emma, " he began. "Emma—can you give me help?"

Even his voice had changed. There was a plaintive tone about it, like the sad songs Father loved to sing.

"Oh, *ja*, Rudi," I answered, trying not to sound too eager. "What with?"

"My English, Emma. Like last year. I need to teach my mother before it is *verboten*—you know, forbidden, to speak *auf deutsch*, in German. *Mein Bruder*, my brother, Winfried, won't help. He's upset with Mutti for not learning English, and me for speaking only German with her. She—we—need your help. Emma."

"I'll help you all I can, Rudi. And maybe my mother can help too. She wants to learn to knippel, to make the beautiful lace your mother makes. Maybe she can speak English with her, then."

Why did I add that? Was I giving my chance away?

"Well, for now, maybe it's better I teach her. She is shy, you know— living in Goosetown—not so well-educated as—as some. She is still an alien, Emma. Didn't think it important to sign up for citizenship. And now, there may be a literacy test for aliens. You see, we need your help. *Bitte?*"

"Oh my, Rudi, I didn't realize. An alien? Oh my. Of course I'll help. Gladly."

"*Gut*. Tomorrow, then. Here?" Rudi asked and smiled. But it wasn't the dazzling smile I remembered four, heavy months ago. Something besides the German language was bothering Rudi Meyerdorf. What could it be?

But he wanted me to help him. I'd get to be with him—alone. Oh, joy!

We met again in the music room after Glee Club. Rudi was serious and distant all the time, trying so hard to listen and learn—both the grammar and the pronunciation. He wanted so much to understand, to do it right, my heart went out to him.

Am I doing it right, I wondered, each time we met? Is he feeling what I'm feeling? Is more than learning to speak good English bothering him—our nearness—our distance—What could I do to make it easier—more fun—more like Vicky?

It came to me one day. I'd teach him some tongue twisters that would help him with the th's that Father had so much trouble with—"Theophilous Thistle, the successful thistle sifter—".

The next time we met, I started with my new idea. I stuck my tongue out between my lips to show him how to sound out the "th."

"Like this?" Rudi asked, sticking his tongue out, right at me. In an instant, before he could say Theophilous, he popped it back in again. Try as he would, he couldn't keep it in the right place.

I covered my mouth to hold back the giggle that bubbled up. "Rudi! Try again. Like this!" And I stuck my tongue out between my lips and breathed— "th —th—th—"

Rudi tried again, and there we stood, facing one another, tongues sticking out right at each other. "Th—th—," we both sounded, forcing our breaths out between our teeth.

I kept blowing gently until I ran out of breath, but Rudi kept right on. "Th—th—"

"No fair, Rudi, you're a trumpet player!" I gasped, laughing and pointing at funny Rudi.

Rudi finally stopped. "Theophilous Thistle," he pronounced, perfectly. "There, teacher, I got it!" And he exploded with a hearty chuckle I had never heard from him before.

A feeling of relief and triumph poured through me, as though I'd just reached the top of Hermann. I wanted with all my heart to run to him and put my arms around him and let us both laugh and cry, together. Such a little thing had just happened. Such a big thing!

Rudi's chuckling faded quickly. He smiled at me, looking directly into my eyes and took a step toward me. I reached my hand behind me, feeling for the edge of the piano to steady myself.

Then, abruptly, Rudi seemed to have changed his mind. He stopped. "Emma, I have to tell you something. I don't want to, but I must."

He shut the book he was still holding with a quick snap, just as he had last spring. Was he going to say this was our last time together—our last lesson? My heart sank.

"I—first—*mein Bruder,* Winfried—I worry about him. He wants to quit school and join the army. My mother is frail. She doesn't take it well—and my brother wants to fight Germans."

Rudi stopped talking abruptly and looked down at his feet.

"*Ja,* Rudi?—"

He struggled to raise his head and look at me. He cleared his throat.

"Well, Emma, there is—how can I say it? I just have to say it—there is much feeling against Germans and, and—you see, I go around in places to play music with small groups and I—I listen. Emma—I hear things."

Rudi hesitated again, looked at me with worry in his eyes and then went on in a rush, "And there is this feeling all around that everything we say is overheard. We are being spied on. It is going around there are spies in town."

"Rudi!" The horrifying scene at the Grossbach came back in a flash. The walls have ears, Father said.

"*Ja,* it is so, Emma. And—I've—strangers ask questions, natural, like—but I know it's not natural—for—for a stranger. They want to know where Karl is. He is a draft dodger, they say. They want to know who is hiding him. Emma, they asked last week about your father! They think he knows. They think he is pro-German. That he may be a spy. They're watching him, Emma. You must warn him!"

"Rudi!" Too unbelievable to understand, too frightening for tears, I turned my back from Rudi and leaned on the piano. He came up behind me and put his hands on my shoulders.

"Please, Emma. *Bitte.* Everybody knows your father is a good man. The people in our town are good people—most of them. We know we have no spies. Nobody talks. Nobody says one word. Not about your father or Fritsche, or Vogel or Pfaender, or any of them. But warn your father, anyway."

I felt the absence of his hands on my shoulders. I heard him walk across the room, open the door, close it softly behind him. But I did not watch him go.

It was on the way home that I began to remember things I hadn't paid much attention to before, things I'd noticed, but forgotten. In my mind I always found a good reason for each thing—or Father had a good reason.

Father had taken more trips than usual to the country to visit the Grossbachs. He hadn't asked Mama and me to go along. But, then, I'd been busy at school, Mama busy in the kitchen, as usual. Oma was totally bed-ridden now and needed his visits. Reasons enough for those trips.

Father still preached peace, forgiveness and love—still, all in German, both morning and evening services and prayer meeting on Wednesday night. But then, that was his religion. Separation of church and state, we'd learned from Mr. Klemm.

Still, I hadn't heard one negative word from him about Germany. No word of praise about the American war effort, even at home. And his many trips to Saint Paul were very mysterious. Father said he went to meetings of the German Methodist Conference to discuss changing the name, dropping the German from German Methodist. He was against it, he said. It's war hysteria, he said. Methodism had made great strides in Germany and that was how Grandfather Altenberg had become Christian. Why should we deny our heritage?

I realized in thinking back that the door to Father's Holy of Holies, which had often been shut, was now shut most of the time and it seemed like he was having lots of conversations he didn't want over-heard. What secrets was he keeping? Was my father helping to hide Karl Grossbach—a draft dodger? That was against the law!

My father couldn't possibly be a spy. I knew in my bones that could not be true. But if he really was helping to hide Karl, and Karl really was a draft dodger, didn't that make my own father a pro-German traitor? How could I warn him that there were rumors he was a spy and was being watched? How could I warn him without telling him exactly where I got the information, which he would surely insist upon. That would mean questions about Rudi and the lessons and more questions about my seeing a boy alone in the music room—a boy who was Catholic? A boy I had feelings about that Father would definitely disapprove of.

But I'd have to find a way to warn him. I had to. Already the men in the black Studebaker knew Father was involved with Karl and the Grossbachs in some way. Would they come roaring up in front of our house any day?

In January, I would have my sixteenth birthday. In two years I would graduate and be going away to college. Father believed in education for women, and I was proud of him for that, for so many things. It was time for me to grow up. Like Victoria, I must learn to talk to my father, question him, maybe even disagree with him, and go against his will.

Question him, yes. But go against his will? Why was it so hard for me? What was I afraid of? Hurting his feelings beyond repair? Disagreeing with him, disappointing him, the one who thought so much of me—loved me so much. Or could it be, could it possibly be I was afraid of something else in him I had never seen before?

Thinking all these miserable thoughts, my torment was more than I thought I could bear. But through all of the conflicting feelings, Rudi's words came back to me.

"They think he is pro-German. They think he is a spy. You must warn him," Rudi had said. And I knew that Rudi was absolutely right. I had to do something.

Supper time was always the best time to talk, before anyone gathered for a meeting, or before the telephone rang.

"I have heard these rumors, too." Father said, when I told him what Mr. Klingman had said about internment. *Es tut mir sehr leid.* It makes me very sad. But I think that it is just a rumor. To frighten us."

"Father—I was wondering—I know you don't like to talk about it—but—how are the Grossbachs?" That was as close as I could get to asking him straight out about his trips to the country, and whether he was helping to hide Karl.

"I tried to reassure Dietrich that he was not a coward. Tried to help him know he is a fine Christian and that the men who assaulted and humiliated him are the ones to feel sorry for. It is war time. Wartime makes fear. Fear makes people do strange things. Ugly things. A fellow pastor from Minneapolis—an elderly gentleman was arrested while working in his garden. Something about a letter to the president. He refused to preach sermons that would help in selling Liberty Bonds. He was accused of wanting to incite the assassination of the president. I knew this pastor when he lived in Sleepy Eye. He was such a mild, gentle soul. He couldn't possibly—"

Mama suddenly stood up and started to pick up the dishes. She asked, "Don't you ever get angry, Christian?"

"*Ja*, sure," Father answered. "There is much anger in me. Don't you hear me in the pulpit sometimes? I get angry at the sin—injustice, cruelty. I get angry at the sinners, too. But what good does it do? There are other ways of fighting evil."

That was Father. Kind. Reasonable. Wise.

Mama gathered the dishes without worrying about how much noise she made. We both had heard these words before.

"Those men!" she sputtered. "Treating Dietrich like that. I bet they had been drinking! Such language!"

"*Komm*, Emma, come." Father said, quickly changing the subject. "We help Mama with the dishes. Then, we sing."

Father's calm reassurance and Mama's indignation were so usual, so familiar, all my fears seem to drift away. It was almost as though the darkness and fear that hung over us all these months lifted, and everything was normal again.

Mama and Father sang duets, while I played piano. Their voices sounded so beautiful together, Mama's rich alto, Father's deep bass voice.

When we finished our music time together, and I climbed the stairs to go to bed. Father called to me. "Don't forget to say your prayers, Emma. For all our loved ones. For peace."

As I lay in bed watching dark clouds move swiftly across the full moon, Rudi came into my mind again. He had been so worried for me, for Father. I had not thanked him for confiding in me about his troubles and about the suspicions of my father. That must have been difficult for him.

I realized, then, Father had not said anything about Karl. Why didn't I ask him straight out? Why didn't I ask him about his trips to Saint Paul? Why had my resolve to warn him dissolved in the strength of his calm reason and faith?

There were no answers in my head. None in the sky that darkened before my eyes. Could I pray as Father asked? What should I pray for? For peace—peace at any price? That we would win the war? That everybody would be safe—Father, Rudi, his mother, his brother, Karl and all the Grossbachs, Mr. Klemm, all those who were suffering anywhere? I made a swift prayer for all of them.

"And please, dear God, don't let my father be a traitor. Forgive me, please, also, for thinking, even for a moment, that he might be!"

Just as I was whispering "Amen," forgotten words came to me. Where had I heard them?

"Lord make me an instrument of Thy peace—"

For the first time in ages, a prayer comforted me. The prayer of Saint Francis—a Catholic prayer. I finished what I remembered, and then fell asleep.

CHAPTER FOURTEEN

Questions of Loyalty

NEWSPAPERS WERE SPREAD out on the library table and the staff of the *Graphos* huddled together over them. The headlines glared up at us.

GERMAN WERHMACHT WINNING ON WESTERN FRONT. Russian Revolution ends conflict there. Thousands of German troops released to fight Allies. Huns using poison gas! Infants bayoneted!

"Just wait until our boys get there!" Walter Ebers said.

My heart began to pound as thoughts bumped around in my head. Infants bayoneted? Germans did that? Huns? How hurtful to Father, if true. If he knew that, would he still defend his *Heitmatland*, his homeland? "War brings out the worst in men," he said. Could my father possibly—? Before I could finish the thought, Walter's voice in interrupted, "Prussian militarists—that's who—"

"I wonder what the German newspapers say about us? We use gas, too," Max said, his voice low and quiet.

"That's disloyal!" Arnold Weiss muttered, not looking at Max, a pink flush creeping up his cheeks. I could feel the tension in the room rising.

I held my breath, praying there would not be another fight. But I didn't say a word. None of us girls said a word.

I glanced over at Amelia. She had turned away from the newspapers and looked down at her hands clasped tightly in her lap. She seemed defeated, like the war was being fought right in front of her and she was losing. How could I be an instrument of peace at a moment like this?

Bertha Brinkmann stood up walked over and put her hand on Max's arm, patting it as she talked. "Sh—sh—. Boys—please—Mr. Klingman says we're not supposed to think—" she hesitated, looked confused. "I mean, I think we should be loyal," she added, lamely. Max sat down slowly, shaking his head.

"Who said anything about being disloyal?" Max answered her, looking at her, his voice much lower, softer than it had been before. She was the only one that could calm Max down.

"It's disloyal to say anything bad about the Allies—anything!" Arnold practically shouted. "We're at war. Mr. Klemm, brothers, cousins, American boys are out there, willing to sacrifice their lives!"

"Does that mean we can't say what we think?" Walter Brunner demanded, his voice rising. "Freedom of speech, we're supposed to have. Can't we—"

Mr. Klingman's sudden presence in the doorway stopped Walter at once. The boys sat down. Our talking stopped, and the room was as silent now as it had been loud the moment before. Mr. Klingman stood there for a moment, saying nothing, a deep scowl on his face. He gathered the newspapers that we had spread all over the table, folded them, put them under the chair and sat down. He pulled his chair in closer to the table. It made a scraping sound in the silenced room.

"You know, ladies and gentleman," he began. "Just a short time ago, you were given permission to have a school paper. Now that you have the opportunity, are you going to spoil it for yourselves by turning these staff meetings into a political debate? I've warned you before. Now, I think you need to turn your energies into making this a good school paper." He pounced on the word *school*.

No one said anything for a long time, and then Bertha spoke up. "I've been thinking," she said. "We should use the *Graphos* to promote the Boys' and Girls' Loyalty class. You know, let the town know we support the Loyalty Oath that's circulating around town. Lots of people have signed it already."

"*Ja*—yes, I mean," Gertrude Hammer added. "We could promote the war work of New Ulm High School—things like the Bread Baking Class to learn how to make bread with ersatz flour, so the boys over there have real flour."

"And Surgical Dressing Classes, things like that. Things that would show we are loyal Americans!" Bertha said.

I looked over at Amelia again, but she was still motionless. Neither of us opened our mouths to add one single thing. I kept wishing one of us would say speak up. Would our loyalty be questioned if we didn't say something?

"Amelia, what do you think? Have you got any ideas?" I asked impulsively, immediately sorry I had opened my mouth. What was the matter with me, putting my friend on the spot like that?

Amelia stirred in her seat for the first time. "Well, I think we should have—have unity!" she said and I could hear the tears in her voice.

"*Ja, Ja*, unity!" I echoed, relieved and grateful Amelia had finally said something. "My mother has a proverb her mother taught her. 'A common enemy makes friends.' All those out there who think New Ulm is disloyal are our common enemy."

All eyes were fastened on me. No one spoke.

"In unity there is strength. *Ja*, that's it," I went on, the words tumbling out. "That could be our watch word. If we believe that, we can get along and work together for the good of everybody."

Mr. Klingman nodded at me, "Well said. Write that. That's what the *Graphos* is all about."

Max stood up. "If we have to keep from speaking the truth to prove we are loyal, we've already lost our freedom. Freedom of speech. Freedom of the press. If those things are not what the *Graphos* is all about, I resign as editor!"

Before anyone could protest, Max picked up his books and left the room. Feelings of dismay and disloyalty flooded me. Did I say something wrong? Should I have kept silent? "Keep silent unless you can think of something better than silence." I looked over at Bertha who covered her lips with her hands.

"Well, staff, I guess you'd better get on with electing a new editor," Mr. Klingman announced without any further reference to Max. No one protested.

On the way home I decided I would have to live with confusion the rest of my life. My mind was a jumble. The whole question of loyalty came to me. Max's words, "Who said anything about disloyalty?" Then I remembered the terrible headlines: Huns using poison gas, bayoneting babies—unspeakable atrocities.

No matter which way I turned, I felt disloyal—to my father on the one hand; on the other to my friends on both sides of the conflict—to the United States of America, my country, my own birth home. What held my deepest loyalty? The Loyalty Oath. Did Father know about it? Had he signed it? What if he hadn't? Would I ask him, please to do so? Would I question his loyalty if I asked? Would he be hurt, insulted, angry, even? Or would he keep calm and reasonable and I'd forget my doubts. I'd never doubted him before in my life. More changing going on inside me? But I had to ask. I had to find a way. I remembered Rudi's warning, "There are spies in town asking about your father."

Rudi. Loyalty to Rudi, too? My head pounded. Why did the grownups have to mess up their world so we couldn't get on with ours?

After supper, before the telephone started to ring, I took a deep breath and plunged ahead. Thinking about Rudi's warning, I told Father about the *Graphos* meeting, our quarrels, and Amelia's plea for unity. Then, I casually brought up the Loyalty Oath.

"*Ja*, Emma, I know about the Loyalty Oath. Many have signed it. Many have not. So many are afraid for their families, their businesses, afraid the whole town might be interned, if they do not sign."

"But why not sign it?" I asked as I thought about the Loyalty Classes at school.

"Many town people are indignant that they have to prove their loyalty. Didn't the governor and others read the speeches at the rally? They ought to know we are a loyal town. It is hurtful to be so doubted. When we tried so hard."

"But Father—if it helps New Ulm?"

"It doesn't help our town to go against our conscience. I didn't sign and will not sign. It is against my beliefs to sign any oath. I know my heart. I know my soul." He sounded angry, rare for him.

Mama walked over to the table with the coffee pot. She filled Father's cup, then her own. "We're asked to do things for the war effort all the time—I'll do what I can—for the soldier boys way over there, even the knitting I hate so much. I'll do it for them—not to prove I'm loyal!" She plunked the pot down on the cast iron trivet, punctuating her announcement. "But one thing I absolutely will not do is change the name of sauerkraut to liberty cabbage. So there!"

The telephone jangled, interrupting our conversation. Father left the table. But I had my answer, leaving me still confused. I can't say I felt satisfied, but I didn't think either Mama or Father had an answer that would make me feel better.

Father came back to the table sooner than usual. He looked at me strangely.

"It's that young man, Emma. Rudi. Rudi Meyerdorf. He sounds upset. He wants you to call him. Here's his number. He's at the Waldheim Cafe."

I couldn't tell from his voice what Father was thinking. Friends from school seldom called one another on the telephone. Rudi didn't even have a telephone at his house. Something must be terribly wrong.

I went in to Father's study. Should I close the door? I wanted to, but I didn't. I turned the little crank, my heart beating furiously. I gave the operator the number.

Rudi answered. "Emma. Emma, it's me, Rudi." As if I didn't know!

"*Was ist los*, what's the matter, Rudi?"

Rudi talked all in a rush, in a way I had never heard before.

"It's my mother, Emma. It's my brother. Gone. Left a note. Wants to join the army. Mutti is upset just terrible. Sits—stares. She is, I'm afraid—soul sick. I can't get our priest, Emma. Your father, a pastor, not Catholic, but kind—your mother, so kind. Could you come? Help us? Could you—*bitte*—please?

"Oh, Rudi, we'll come. For sure. We'll be there right away!"

I put the receiver back on the hook and rushed to the kitchen, Rudi's urgent message and request tumbling out all at once.

Father crumpled his napkin and stood up from the table. "Of course we'll go!"

"Poor Frau Meyerdorf," Mama said, shaking her head as she followed Father to get her coat without even picking up the dishes.

Father and Mama, I thought gratefully. I may not always understand them, but they can be counted on to help when someone's in trouble. I grabbed my own coat and followed my parents out the door.

CHAPTER FIFTEEN

Goosetown

FATHER CRANKED UP our Ford car. We climbed in, all three of us, and were on our way in moments that seemed like an eternity, my heart beating like a big drum. My thoughts careened all over inside me. Mama and Father! How sure I had been that they would both respond to a call for help—no matter who was calling. I'd never been inside a house in Goosetown before. I had never been inside a Catholic house! But I would get to see Rudi! Rudi was in trouble. His mother—was she going crazy? But I would get to be with Rudi—in his own home!

We crossed the tracks. We were in Goosetown, where the Bohemian Germans lived in their neat houses painted different colors, pink, blue, pale green—not the red brick with white painted porches on our side of the tracks. There was the river glittering in the late autumn sunlight through the trees, almost bare of leaves. There were the small barns behind the houses and the empty lots with white geese nibbling the last of the summer seeds. *Gänzeviertel*—Goosetown, beloved by the Germans from Bohemia. Another world inside our world, half country, half town. I wished I could see it in summer when all the flowers the Bohemians loved so much were in bloom. I wondered if I ever could.

Mama knew the house, Rudi's house, and we climbed out of the car, went up the steps and rang the bell.

Rudi met us at the door. Here, in his own surroundings, he looked more like a boy, not so princely as at school or in the Hofmeister Band, but tired and hurting. I wanted to run to him right away as I did when Father looked hurt.

We walked into the small parlor, neat as a pin, handmade lace-trimmed curtains at the windows, a carved wooden crucifix hanging on the wall opposite the door. I had never seen a crucifix up close before. It seemed so strange.

Rudi's mother sat in a chair, twisting her lace-trimmed handkerchief round and round. She was staring out of the window, looking frightened. She didn't seem to notice our presence. She didn't say anything, just sat there, twisting her kerchief and staring, unseeing, it seemed. Mama went right over to her, bent down, and put her arms around her.

"Frau Meyerdorf, *was ist los?* What's the trouble?"

Rudi's mother didn't answer. It was as though she hadn't heard. Finally, Rudi broke the silence.

"It's my brother Winfried—Winnie," he said. "Mutti, my mother, has always worried about him. Now he wants to join the army. He's just a boy. Too young. He started to leave the house this afternoon and Mutti hung on to him, crying—and—and he hit her! And—and he slammed the door shut and left the house. He hasn't come home since. Mutti keeps looking for him. A while ago, Mutti stopped crying, and she just sits there, like she was—was gone, too! I tried to call the priest, but—"

There was no time for anyone to answer Rudi. The back door banged and the tall, wild looking boy I knew as Winnie Meyerdorf stormed into the parlor. He was taller than Rudi, but looked younger. Mama would have said not yet dry behind the ears.

"Winnie, you're back!" Rudi exclaimed and reached for his brother.

Winnie pushed him away. "Don't call me Winnie! What kind of a name is that? Winfried! Means peace? I hate peace. I hate my German name. It's a girl's name in America. I hate Germany and being German-American. From now on my name's Larry! Larry Meyers. A good American name."

He started to turn away and then came back toward his brother. He made a fist and held out his arm. "If I could," he said between his teeth. "I'd slit my wrists and squeeze out every drop of German blood!"

Rudi started to take another step toward Winfried—Larry.

Larry backed away, violence in every tense muscle. "And leave your hands off me—both you and Ma!"

He glared at Mama and Father and then, at me, like he saw us for the first time. He blurted, "What are you doing here, anyway? You're not a priest! And I wouldn't talk to any old priest, anyway."

Thank goodness Father did not go to Winfried—Larry. He just stood there and calmly said, "We were worried about your mother. We came to see her."

Larry looked over at his mother and our eyes followed his. Mutti was still sitting motionless, except for the twisting handkerchief, Mama sitting quietly beside her, patting the twisting fingers.

Larry started to move toward his mother, then hesitated. "Oh, she always gets a spell when she's mad at me." And with that he stalked off into another room and shut the door.

What could anyone say? Or do? Rudi looked so uncomfortable, I thought I'd die.

Father came to the rescue. "Rudi, your mother does need care. The hospital, maybe, for a little while."

"Oh, please, *bitte*, Reverend. Not the hospital. They'd send her off to the crazy house in Saint Peter and I'd never see her again. I was wrong. Winnie—Larry, was right. She has these spells often when she's upset and gets over them. Please, *mein Herr*, leave her with me. Let me take care of her. When the priest comes back, he'll come. She always does well with Father Lempke. I shouldn't have bothered you. I'm sorry."

Rudi was so earnest and looked so uncomfortable, I was sure Father felt we would do the right thing to leave. This was a Catholic matter, now. I wanted to leave, not wanting to embarrass Rudi any more. Yet another part of me wanted so much to stay and help him. Be near him.

"Well, son," my father said. "*Danke schön.* Thank you for calling us. Feel free to call again any time you can't reach Father Lempke."

"If you need me—" Mama said.

"Rudi—I—. Thanks for calling," I stammered.

"Thank you for coming. I was upset," Rudi said as he took us to the door.

The car was quiet on the way home. I was glad. I was glad, too, that Father hadn't said, "Let's have a word of prayer," because I wasn't sure he knew how to pray Catholic.

Mama did say one of her German proverbs, "When you put out another's candle, you will also be in the dark."

We rode on in silence. I wasn't sure I understood that proverb.

Just before we got home, Father spoke for the first time. "I hope Father Lempke knows what to do. Winnie may need discipline, but too much may drive him further away. Something more than being German-American is bothering that young man. And Frau Meyerdorf doesn't need to be told the devil is in her."

"Well, not all Catholic priests think that way, Father," I managed to say, feeling somehow I had to defend Catholics, even though I didn't know anything about them.

"That may very well be," Father answered. And that was all that was said.

It took me a long time to go to sleep that night, remembering the scene in Rudi's house. In my mind's eye, I saw the crucifix on the wall, his silent mother, his angry brother.

It was all so strange. It was as though that in crossing the tracks into Goosetown, we passed into another world, making the distance between Rudi and me even greater. But, then, I remembered Rudi's face and I ached for him. In some ways I felt more distant from him than I ever had before. In another way, I felt much closer.

Would Rudi feel the same? Would he be so embarrassed by our witnessing his family secrets that he wouldn't want to see me again? Then I remembered the All-School Picnic. He had seen my fear. He'd seen me throw up. And it didn't seem to make any difference.

I finally got to sleep and didn't dream of falling or of floating on a cloud. I didn't dream at all. Waking life was difficult enough these days. I didn't need frightening nightmares.

CHAPTER SIXTEEN

Froh Weihnachten

BEFORE I OPENED my eyes a few weeks after the trip to Goosetown, I knew that it was snowing. The early December morning was still black, so I couldn't see the white flakes drifting down, but I could feel the snowy presence. There was a certain hush in the air. Snow flakes fall so silently, cover the bare ground so gently, that it was easy to believe this dark morning that all our fears and all our sorrows were being tenderly covered with a downy blanket.

I walked the eight blocks to school in the snow, holding my books close to me under my coat, sticking out my tongue to catch a flake or two. The first snows always reminded me of Christmas. It would be coming soon, with all its excitement and sense of wonder. Nothing in the world, I was sure, was quite like a German Christmas—the tree, the music, the special fragrances—anise and cinnamon and balsam fir. A Christmas-is-coming thrill poured through me.

And then, a thud. A few more weeks, and school would be out for Christmas vacation. I probably wouldn't be seeing Rudi for fifteen long days. We were at war. The Glee Clubs would not be singing German Christmas carols. This year we would not hear *Stille Nacht*, Silent Night. And how could Mama bake seventeen kinds of German Christmas cookies—*springerlie, lebkucken, pfeffernüss*, without sugar and flour, now that it was unpatriotic to use what the boys over seas needed so much. How long was this dreadful war going to last? How long was New Ulm going to live under this blanket of gloom and fear?

Two more blocks to school. There, at least, I would see Rudi and Victoria and my other friends and we could talk about basketball and boys and the play Victoria was in and what to do with our hair in winter.

And I would see Rudi! This was "our day"—Glee Club practice day and our English lesson afterwards. It was always good to be near him, even though he'd seemed sad and serious ever since our visit to his home. He had thanked me again for coming that night, but when I asked about his mother, he'd only answered briefly. "She's better. Father Lempke came and said a rosary with her and fingering the beads seemed to make her feel better."

I hadn't seen his brother in school and I hated to ask about him. Where was he now, I wondered.

Then, Karl came to my mind as I walked along. Where was he? What would he do for Christmas? Would he be all alone and cold in the far away North Woods? If that's where he really was. And Mr. Klemm. Would he be crouched in some mud-filled trench as far away from Christmas as a human being could be? And Father. What was he really thinking—and doing—these troubling days?

Try as I would, and in spite of the beautiful snow, I couldn't get the war off my mind and the way it was affecting our whole town, not only Father, but all the rest of New Ulm, it seemed. And especially Rudi, his mother, his brother. They were all tangled together in one big worry.

It was still barely light when I got to school, eager to hear the voices of my friends chattering to one another trying to keep things ordinary.

But the moment I stepped into the hall, I knew from the atmosphere that things were not ordinary.

"Did you hear the news?" Bertha whispered to me as we were hanging up our coats and shaking the snow from our boots. A group of girls had gathered round, and as we bent over, taking off our boots, we kept whispering as though the walls did have ears, as Father had said.

"What news?" I whispered back. There was so much these days. Could they have heard about Winnie Meyerdorf? Larry Meyers,

that is. Had someone heard about Karl before we did? Mr. Klemm, I
thought! He's been wounded!

"Dr. Fritsche has been removed from office—for sedition! Pfaender,
too! By the Governor and the Minnesota Commission for Public
Safety! We may all be interned—the whole town!"

"Vicky's father? Dr. Becker? Him, too?" I managed to ask.

"I don't know. I don't think so," Bertha answered, still whispering.

At that very moment, Victoria came stomping in and shook the
snow off her coat, letting it fly all over. She had a look on her face like
the one Mama got when she was indignant.

"That commission!" she sputtered, no trace of a whisper in her voice.
"Removed from office without any say-so from us whatsoever. After
dragging it out so long. Keeping us so worried. One way they could
make an issue of New Ulm to the whole state!"

"Vicky—your father?" Bertha and I both asked out loud at the same
time.

"No, not yet, anyway. Maybe the Commission didn't think he was
important enough," she answered, jamming her coat on the hook.
"Imagine, calling these men traitors, seditious. It's ridiculous. It's
unconstitutional! Why, those men, and my father, too, are as loyal as
red, white and blue! How can they do that? This is our town! Is this a
democracy, or not?"

I gave Vicky a quick hug. "What is happening to us?" I managed to
ask, my question hanging in the air, unanswered by anyone.

Vicky smiled wanly at me as the bell rang, calling us to our first
class. Before we went our separate ways, we hugged each other, all
of us, those who had favored the war, those who had not. Some of
the boys came by as we stood there and gave us a friendly tap on the
shoulder. Walter Ebers walked by, stopped, opened his mouth to say
something; then shook his head, gave Vicky's shoulder a squeeze and
walked on.

I hurried down the hall, my thoughts racing. I was relieved about
Vicky's father, but our own beloved mayor, Dr. Fritsche, Vogel, and
Pfaender—these good, honest men removed from the offices our

town had elected them to? I remembered their faces at the All-School Picnic, already hurt and discouraged about their reception in Washington, before the rally. And now! Dismissed from office?"

My heart ached. I thought about Father again. What would he do, how would he feel if he were dismissed from his beloved church, or if the German Methodist Church were outlawed? And internment—the whole town—men, women, children—was that really possible? Would they huddle us all together in some small space somewhere and then fence us in, somehow. I tried to picture our whole town out on the cold prairie, enclosed in barbed wire. Could our government do that? Stories had reached us of Germans, artists, musicians, from the East Coast being interned in some kind of camp in the South. Thousands, we'd heard. How many aliens were there in New Ulm? An icy chill ran up my spine. Fear—that's the word Frau Becker used. Anger, bewilderment first—then fear.

In school we disagreed about so many things, shouted at each other, resigned from jobs and walked away from each other, like Max from the *Graphos* staff. Now, facing a common enemy, we were together. I remembered those brief moments in the hall—how we hugged each other and gave encouraging shoulder taps to other boys and girls. Unity, Amelia said. Maybe the whole town would respond with the same mutual support and concern. Even in our shock and pain and anger and fear, all of New Ulm might unite as a community.

The day went much faster then I would have dreamed. Although my head spun all day thinking of all that was going on in our town, when I saw Rudi, all my hurt and fear faded away. There he was, standing in the tenor section of the Glee Club, but looking especially grave and troubled. It was a struggle getting through practice as I kept seeing the worried look on his face. Looking at him, I knew that for once I would not be devastated if he could not stay for our lesson after practice. But he did.

I didn't know whether to ask about his mother, or not. I didn't know whether to smile, or not. I just stood there as he came up to me. I reached out my hand to touch him, then drew it back. He looked so solemn, so sad.

"Oh, Rudi, is your mother—" I managed to ask.

"She is—" he began, hesitated, then went on. "There is something I must tell you. Father Lempke took Mutti and me to the recruiting office in Mankato to tell them my brother was too young to enlist. But it was too late. Winnie had registered as Larry Meyers, lied about his age, I guess, and they sent him to Texas to be shipped out. Mutti went quiet again. Father Lempke had to take her to the hospital— not Saint Peter, but here—the Loretto Hospital. I've never seen my mother so bad."

"Oh, Rudi," That's all I could think of to say. I felt helpless.

"I need to go to the hospital, Emma, so I can't stay for our lesson today."

He turned to go without another word and I swallowed the lump in my throat. Then, at the door, he turned and looked at me.

"I was wondering, Emma," he said, "if sometime you would like to go to Holy Trinity Church with me. Sometime, during Christmas time. I'll say a rosary for my mother and my brother and you can see Holy Trinity. It is very beautiful. You would like it, I think."

My hand flew to my throat. To cover my pulse, to quiet it a little. The Catholic Church? And me, a Methodist minister's daughter? I couldn't let him know how shocked I was. I couldn't go, of course. Father would not allow it.

"Oh, Rudi," I heard myself say, "That's wonderful. That's just wonderful. I—I think I would like that very much."

He smiled, almost the same dazzling smile I remembered and hadn't seen for so long. He turned away from me then, and walked out the door, leaving me with the greatest dilemma of my life, so far.

CHAPTER SEVENTEEN

The Dilemma Deepens

WHEN WOULD I ask Father? Mama? That seemed to be all I thought about in the few days before school let out. Why was it so hard? In my head I practiced what I to say and how to say it. A simple, casual statement would be best—at the supper table. Calmly, I would look them in the eyes and say, "Rudi wants me to go to Holy Trinity Church with him, while he says a rosary for his mother."

But the dark look on Father's face when he disapproved of something, and worst of all, his look of hurt and disappointment that would be there when I made my announcement, and it was more than I thought I could stand. Not now. Not when he was already so troubled. And what if he said flatly, "No! No, my dear, that would not be a good idea?" What would I do then?

So the few supper times before Christmas vacation slipped by as we talked about the dismissal from office of Fritsche and Pfaender, about New Ulm's possible internment, about the Beckers and the Grossbachs, until there was only one chance left, one supper time only for me to make my simple, causal statement.

"Emma, you're not touching your supper," Mama said, looking disapprovingly at my half-filled plate.

"Oh," I answered casually, my stomach full of butterflies. I thought about the Meyerdorf's too. "Did you hear about Frau Meyerdorf—that she's in the hospital—at Loretto? Father Lempke took her there after they learned Larry had been sent to Texas for training?"

Father's penetrating look lasted for only a moment and then he shook his head sadly, "*Ja,* I heard and I'm grateful she is being cared for in a good Catholic hospital. Those Catholics. They certainly stick together. Wish we Protestants could do the same." That was all he said, crumpling his napkin and leaving the table for his Holy of Holies.

So my last chance was gone and I hadn't mentioned Rudi's invitation to visit Holy Trinity to say a prayer for his mother and brother. What kind of coward was I? What was I so afraid of, really? What was I going to do now?

Rudi and I had our last brief time together. It was time to say good-bye for two weeks. He told me, "I have a few evenings free, Emma. No band or orchestra practice with Hofmeister. I'll be going to Holy Trinity one of those times. Mondays—Wednesdays are free. Could you come? Seven o'clock?"

That was it! Wednesday. Prayer meeting night! I could meet Rudi and go to his church with him and come home and go to bed without Mama and Father even knowing about it. I wouldn't have to ask. I'd just go!

"Oh, *ja*, Rudi. Wednesday would be fine. I'll meet you there. I may be a little late. Is that all right?"

"No problem. Wednesday isn't Mass. We'll just go in and pray. Be sure to wear something on your head. Well, you'd do that anyway, wouldn't you? You'll like Holy Trinity. It's very beautiful."

It was done. I'd made my choice. Now, I would have to live it out, come what may. Nothing could stop me now from meeting Rudi Meyerdorf in front of Holy Trinity Church a little after seven-thirty Wednesday night, December 23, 1917.

I felt like the spies we'd heard so much about—shadowy characters who snuck around town, eavesdropping on conversations and doing secretive, undercover things.

The most difficult thing I had ever done in my life was to eat supper slowly that night, casually talk about Christmas at our church, but not seem to be in a hurry for Father and Mama to leave for prayer meeting. I offered to help with the dishes, and told them I had to stay home to work on my essay, "Why I Am Proud To Be An American."

It all went so well, I wanted to say a prayer of thanks, but didn't think

God would listen this time. I heard the sound of singing coming from our church as I hurried by—German Christmas carols. No one—no war—no Minnesota Commission for Public Safety could talk Father into giving those up.

It was snowing again, a beautiful snow. A lovely glow from the stained glass windows of the Catholic church fell on the pure whiteness. Rudi was there, waiting. My ears were so filled with heart poundings, I could barely hear him whisper, *"Guten abend.* Good evening, Emma."

He took me by the arm, opened the heavy doors for me and we walked in. Awe and wonder took my breath away. Never in all my born days had I seen anything like this. It must be like the great cathedrals in Europe I knew only through books and magazines.

Great columns, pure white as the snow that was falling outside rose up and arched above me, making me feel smaller than I ever had in my life. The columns were touched with gold. Lamp light flickered in niches along the sides with statues of saints and the Mother Mary everywhere; and up above the altar, painted in deep rich colors were larger than life images of all the apostles.

Now, I really couldn't breath. It was all so strange, so beautiful, so hushed and mysterious and here was Rudi, a living, breathing young man standing so close beside me. I was sure it was more than I could endure. I feared I would faint—or worse, lose my supper.

I watched Rudi dip his fingers in the holy water and cross himself. He had told me that I didn't need to do the same. He guided me into a pew and knelt, crossed himself. I sat down, feeling awkward, ill at ease, still awed by the strange grandeur around me and Rudi so close beside me. The war in the world and the war inside me seemed unreal. I wanted to stay forever and let the beauty and peace seep into me.

Then, another part of me surfaced. I wanted to run out of here and hurry home to the small, warm, familiar comfort of our little house, our little church, the lusty singing of familiar hymns. I wanted to ask God's forgiveness for being so moved in a Catholic church. I wanted to ask Father's forgiveness for deceiving, betraying him, doubting him.

But what was it about Catholics that Father seemed to fear? What was it about German-Americans everybody in the whole United States seemed to be so afraid of and hated so much?

A shoulder touched mine. Rudi's. I sat motionless as I felt his presence. He was sitting so quietly beside me. My whole insides trembled and yet, I felt comforted, too. Was it Rudi, or the Catholic church? Strange.

I looked at Rudi out of the corner of my eye as he fingered the rosary whispering words I couldn't quite hear or understand. How could I ever fear or doubt this warm, wonderful boy. As he sat praying, did his thoughts wander, like mine? Just because he was Catholic and I was Protestant, were we really so different inside? He was worried about his mother, I was worried about my father.

My thoughts kept tumbling around in my head. I wasn't sure I should be praying in a Catholic church. Still and all, prayer was prayer, wasn't it? "Lord, make me an instrument of Thy peace," was all that came to me.

After a long while, he stood up and guided me out of the sanctuary. "How did you like it?" he asked when we had walked silently away from the glow of the church light into the darkness of the empty street.

"Oh, Rudi—It was beautiful! Just beautiful!"

"I thought you'd like it. Thank you for coming with. And *Froh Weihnachten*, Merry Christmas," he said. We walked on, side by side, without another word. Just before we reached the corner to our house, Rudi stopped. He took my shoulders gently and turned me to him. Even in the darkness, I could see the outline of his face drawing slowly, slowly toward mine. He took my face in his mittened hand, bent down and touched my lips firmly with his own. Then, he released me.

I thought I'd die. Truly. I couldn't open my eyes. I couldn't breath. Rudi's warm lips were gone from mine, but the kiss was still there—

coursing down my arms, surrounding my heart, flooding all of me with strange and overwhelming feelings. This was no courtly kiss on the hand. This was—

"Emma!" I heard Rudi breathe and felt his hands on my shoulders. I opened my eyes, feeling foolish and half scared.

"Yes, Rudi?"

"Emma—I—I—want to thank you for coming. I—well, *Froh Weihnachten!*"

I couldn't see his face clearly, but I thought he wanted to tell me more. But he just patted my shoulder, turned and started to walk away.

"*Froh Weihnachten*, Rudi!" I called after him. But he didn't turn around and just walked on. There was nothing to do, but turn in the opposite direction toward home.

The lights in our little church were still on. Thank the Lord, I'd gotten home before prayer meeting was over. I carefully hid my snowy coat in the back closet. I crept up the stairs, in case Father and Mama should walk in before I was in bed. I was in no mood to talk to them. To anybody, this night.

I put on my nightie and sat up in bed. I lit a candle and for the first time in ages, picked up the treasure box from the night stand beside my bed that held special mementos from my childhood. I opened it.

There was a rabbit's foot Karl Grossbach had given me long ago, a tiny gold locket with my baby picture in it, a tuft of baby hair tied with a pink ribbon, a twig of bittersweet, my first sachet the Beckers had given me. Nothing from Rudi. Nothing but memories. Is that all I would ever have? I touched my lips with my finger tips, dipped my fingers into the box as I had seen Rudi do with the holy water, kissed my finger tips and closed the box. Then, I lay down, closed my eyes and willed the memory of this night to stay with me forever.

CHAPTER EIGHTEEN

Christmas Eve

"AND MARY KEPT all these things and pondered them in her heart."

Father closed the German Bible he had been reading from and the three of us sat in silence looking at our beautiful Christmas tree, carefully watching the burning candles so they wouldn't flicker out, or set fire to a fragrant branch of balsam fir. We enjoyed each fragile ornament, the violins, the little animals, the tiny tea pot I loved best. A few gifts, wrapped in white tissue paper sat under the tree, waiting for the time of silence to pass when we would open our presents and have our Christmas Eve gift sharing, our *Bescherung.*

We had the Christmas Eve service in our plain little church with all the children and mothers and fathers and cousins and *Tantes* and *Onkels* and *Grossmutters* and *Grossvaters.* And there had been singing, and verse speaking and the Bible story and a Santa Claus passing out a little candy to the children. And there had been warm embraces and *Fröhliche Weihnachtens* and all the excitement and warmth of a family Christmas Eve at church, just as if there were no war. Then we had gone our way, each to our own home.

Now we three Altenbergs were alone, with each of us pondering something different, I was sure. Father most likely thought about his Christmas sermon on the real meaning of Christmas, the hope of peace on earth and good will toward men.

What would Mama be thinking? About Mary, the mother of Jesus, being great with child, making her seem human, like all women everywhere? Or would she be thinking that there was only one kind of Christmas cookie this year, made with ersatz flour. I knew so little, really, about my very own mother.

I pondered many things. Rudi, first, and the transporting moment in the softly falling snow, when I had been given my first real kiss.

Mama's voice startled me out of my thoughts. She wasn't saying any of the things I thought she would say. Her voice was very soft and low.

"I can't help thinking about the Grossbachs." she said. "They weren't in church. They must miss Karl, worrying about him. And all those boys that are spending their first Christmas away from home. Christmas is home to me. Without home and family, Christmas can be the loneliest time of the year, I would think. I've never been without family at Christmas."

I looked at Mama, thinking, thinking. Who is this woman, my mother? She was thinking about somebody besides herself. Had I ever really seen my mother? I gazed at my mother, her round face, her thick dark brown hair braided and wrapped across the top of her head, like a crown.

Then, I heard Father's voice, "Young boys on both sides of this terrible war will be lonely. We must not forget that. If the American people want to rid themselves of everything German, they will have to eliminate most of Christmas customs—the tree, many carols, so many things."

I turned my gaze from my mother and looked at my father, saw his sad face and my pondering began again. He certainly seemed to always be defending the Germans, Yet how could I possibly hurt this wonderful man. How could I doubt him, deceive him, betray him? And yet, how could I tell him about the most treasured moment of my life, so far, and bring down an anger that I had seldom seen, but that he had told us was often there. Or worse yet, the look of great, painful disappointment.

I had to tell him sometime, before someone said, "I saw the Methodist minister's daughter in Holy Trinity Church with the Meyerdorf boy." The thought terrified me. I couldn't tell him now. It was Christmas. I couldn't spoil Christmas. And so, I remained silent.

"And the little animals that we roll out on our *springerlie* cookies,"

Mama added. "Those are part of it, too. Animals, like in the stable. I'd like to know how many *springerlie* and *lebkucken* there are in New Ulm this Christmas—war or no war."

I tried with every fiber of my being to direct my thoughts in this room, with Father and Mama, on Christmas Eve, Rudi or no Rudi. War or no war. I had to get into the conversation, somehow. So, I tried.

"The Beckers have a Christmas tree," I said, "and there's a huge tree in Turner Hall and the Turners aren't even Christian—even if they are German."

I felt, rather than saw, Mama's back straighten right out of the soft mood of a moment ago. Was she going to have a little fit, now, on Christmas Eve? She glared at me and said, "What do you mean they aren't Christian? You can't tell me Rosa Becker isn't Christian. What is a Christian, anyway? Somebody who talks about it all the time, or somebody who acts like a Christian—does Christian things, like helping people."

Mama was definitely not afraid of Father, that was one thing you could say about her. She said what she thought, straight out, plain, just as Victoria had said. I could use some of that courage, just now, I thought.

"Oh, Mama," I burst out, "I think you're right. I think everybody, I mean everybody, in this town is celebrating Christmas this night—Methodists, Lutherans, agnostics, Turners—even Catholics! Holy Trinity is open every night."

There! It was out. I caught my breath, looking from Mama to Father, saw them both looking back at me, not saying a word. It was Mama who rescued me, this time. After a small silence her straight back relaxed, and she smiled at me, "You're right, Emma. Elsa Meyerdorf certainly is a good Christian woman and she needs our prayers this Christmas. And that's a fine young man there, that Rudi. The way he looks after his mother. If only those Bohemian Catholics didn't drink so much."

Father was still looking at me, a little frown wrinkling his forehead.

"You seem to be having quite an interest in Catholics lately, Emma," he said.

The time had come. This would not be the same kind of confession I knew the Catholics did, but it would be a confession, just the same. But would it be a relief? I would let something precious out of my treasure box, opening it up to criticism, scorn, anger—something so special. Why did all of this make me so filled with fear, why did it silence me? Confusing, *unwirklich*. I felt paralyzed, struggled to think of something to say, feeling Father's gaze on me, waiting for some response from me.

"Why, *ja*—" I began to say. "We go to school with them, everyday, you see, and they do all the things with us—sports—Glee Club —".

Would I have gone on, if fate hadn't intervened, rescuing me once more? Just at that moment, there was a fierce banging on the back door. Father got up, a puzzled look on his face. Mama and I just sat there looking at each other, wondering who would come banging on our door on Christmas Eve?

From the doorway, we heard a voice, deep and troubled, mumbling.

"*Ach mein Gott in Himmel!* Oh my God in Heaven," we heard Father say. "Karl! Karl Grossbach! *Komm herein. Komm herein.* Come in. Come in!"

CHAPTER NINETEEN

The Return

THE BOYISH TUFT of hair at the back of his head was gone. The sun-burn was gone. A straggly, reddish-brown beard covered his chin. His eye-brows, caked with snow, had bushed out. How could Father have recognized this transformed man standing before us, stomping his feet, tattered, snow-covered stocking cap in his hands.

Mama rushed to him, hugging him, dirty jacket and all. "*Ach*, Karl come in—take your jacket off—your boots. Get off those dirty, wet clothes."

"*Ja*, Karl, Father echoed. "Come in where it's warm."

Mama and Father hovered around Karl as if he was their own long-lost son and Karl did not resist. I stood rooted to the spot, staring at the stranger in front of me, while Father pulled up a chair, gently pushed Karl into it and started to take off his boots.

"Your feet, Karl!" Father exclaimed, "They're white—frost bit. Emma get the wash basin—water—cold. He must put his feet in cold water."

"Emma, get the wash boiler. Fill it up. Karl needs a warm bath. Get your Father's robe, too. Karl, have you eaten?"

Mama, Father and Karl, all three, seemed to have forgotten that I was not Karl's sister as they started to help him undress. I was glad to do something to help so I could leave the kitchen. I got the wash boiler from the back porch, set it on the back of the stove, filled it with enough water for a sponge bath and ran upstairs to get Father's bathrobe. I gathered a pair of father's long underwear, clean socks, and slippers. There was an intimacy in touching these personal things that made me feel I was truly Karl's sister.

I handed the clean clothes through the kitchen door, went back into the living room to sit on the couch and gaze at our beautiful tree.

I picked up a book to read and waited. We still had not opened our presents. I still had not greeted my long lost brother.

Mumbling voices and the fragrance of bacon frying came from the kitchen and a long hour later, a new, clean-shaven Karl came slip-sliding into the living room in Father's slippers, wrapped in Father's flannel robe. He was led by Father, Mama trailing behind, carrying a tray of hot coffee and *snitzbrot*, our German Christmas bread. Karl looked at me, looked down at the jersey underwear sticking out below the robe and grinned at me, the broadest, warmest grin I had ever seen on his face.

I clasped my hands and hugged them to me in my excitement, wanting to hug Karl, not sure it was right, he in a bathrobe and underwear. "Karl, you're back! This is the best Christmas in the whole, wide world!"

"*Ja*, I'm back. Couldn't stay away. Not at Christmas. I thought of my family, mother, father, my sister and little brothers. I wanted to see them."

"*Ja*," Mama said. "For sure."

"See," he said, changing the subject suddenly and lifting his slippered feet in the air. "Not frozen at all, just a little frost bit. Hurt like sin thawing out, but I had worse."

We all laughed a little, sipped our coffee, nibbled our *snitzbrot*, laced with snippets of dried fruit and nuts, and smiled warmly at each other from time to time. None of us questioned Karl any further. I was relieved. Even Mama, usually so forthright and curious, didn't question him.

Karl took his last sip of coffee, refused another cup, and put down his spoon. "I thought of going to Canada. Some boys are going there. Then I thought of all those other boys overseas at Christmas, and I couldn't. I didn't want old Onkel Paul to get into trouble hiding me, either. The nearer Christmas came—I couldn't run away—I had to come home. You understand?"

"*Ja, ja*, we do," Mama nodded, vigorously.

"So I hitch-hiked and caught a freight train. And now I am here."

"*Ja?*" Father asked, and waited for Karl to go on.

"I've decided, Onkel Chris. I've—I've decided to register for the draft. More than that. I've decided, up there in the woods all alone with only Onkel Paul, that I'd—"

"*Ja?*" Mama asked, leaning toward Karl.

Karl squared his shoulders. "I am going to enlist! I am an American—German parentage, true—but American born. It's not the war—that I believe in it—it's that I can't let my American brothers be over there alone."

Grandmother Altenberg's clock ticked loudly in the room.

Father bowed his head, looked at his feet, crossed his hands over his knees, said nothing.

"Maybe you could do something for the Red Cross over there. So you wouldn't have to—you know—shoot German boys, cousins, maybe?" Mama finally said.

"Maybe."

"Before you graduate?" I managed to ask. "Before the Prom and all that?"

"Well, I'll register and see. I'm more than old enough. First, I have to tell Father. He'll be—Onkel Chris, I need your help. That's why I came here first. It's not that I am afraid. Its just so hard to explain. And Oma—she'll be heart-broken."

It took Father a long time before he lifted his head and looked at Karl. "I trust you know what you are doing—that you have prayed about this?"

"I have, Onkel Chris. I have. I hate going against my father's will. But I must, this time."

"Well, then," Father finally answered, patting his knees and standing up. "I go with you. But tomorrow, after you've slept."

"*Danke*, Onkel Chris. Thank you. I so want to see Oma and my mother and Amelia and my little brothers for Christmas."

"I'll light the kerosene heater in the spare room and get you extra covers," Mama said and started for the stairs.

Father patted Karl on the shoulder. "*Gute nacht*, good night, Karl.

Fröhliche Weihnachten. Gott segnet, God bless." He turned and went in to the Holy of Holies shutting the door behind him.

Karl and I were alone now, facing each other. With out a moment's hesitation, I held out my arms to him. He gathered me to him, folded me against his chest and I laid my head against it.

"I love you, brother Karl," I said.

"I love you, little sister," he answered.

"Bed's ready, Karl," Mama called from upstairs.

Karl released me from his warm embrace, held his hand against my cheek for a moment and went upstairs. I picked up the coffee cups and took them to the kitchen, looking back at our tree, candles snuffed out, Christmas gifts still unopened.

It was Christmas afternoon and Karl was still sleeping. Mama had wrapped a towel around a warm brick for his feet and tucked him in like he was the little boy she never had. We went to bed ourselves and got up early for the Christmas Day service at church, where Father preached on his favorite text, "Peace On Earth and Goodwill Toward All Men."

"And the angels sang," he finished, dropping his voice so you had to strain to hear him. "And they will continue to sing, if we will but listen."

Karl stayed home to sleep, which Mama thought he needed more than greeting a congregation full of questions about his disappearance and re-appearance. Andreas Weiss and his family had come to church in a sleigh and were happy to take Karl and Father out to the Grossbach's. They had been gone for hours.

Mama picked up her knitting, even though it was a holy day. Her needles clicked as she frowned and said, "I do hope Dietrich will not be too hard on Karl. He can be a stern father. He's one of those who believes that little verse, *'Was der Vater will, was die Mutter spricht, das befolge still! Warum? Frage nicht!'* Remember?"

"I remember. 'What the father wills and the mother asks, that obey.

Silently. Why? Don't ask!' But I though it was a joke you and Father said to me."

"A joke for some. Not all."

"What will he do, Mama? What can he do? Karl's a grown man."

"Still, a son, Emma. Dietrich can freeze him out. Dead silence, you know. For years, maybe."

In the late afternoon, it was already dark when I heard the sound of sleigh bells coming closer to the house, and then stop. I pulled back the curtains and looked out. Father stepped down from the sleigh while the driver held the lantern for him. It was Onkel Grossbach, and even in the dim light, I saw the grim lines and shadows on his face. He drove off without coming in.

"Coffee, Christian?" Mama asked, "Warmed over Christmas dinner? Sauerkraut and goose? You must be hungry."

"*Nein, danke,* no thank you. I have no appetite."

"Well, maybe a little milk noodle soup."

Milk noodle soup was our comfort food and Mama soon had enough for all three of us. The goose could wait. As we ate our hot milk noodle soup with salt and pepper and lots of butter, Father filled us in on what had happened at the farm. It was a story of tears and questions and warm embraces and more tears. When he finished, he took off his glasses, wiped them with his handkerchief and blew his nose.

"That's a fine young man, that Karl. His father should be proud of him. I disagree with his decision to enlist, but he didn't back down. It will take Dietrich a long time to get over this. Years, maybe. Never, maybe. If something should happen to Karl—I just don't know—."

"Who will help Dietrich farm? If he doesn't farm, the warmongers will accuse him of purposely not raising crops for the army. I heard that from the Red Cross lady."

"That came up. Karl could be deferred to help farm, but he wants to enlist. The neighbors will pitch in. I'll even go out and help. My father farmed when we first came to this country."

Father shook his head and put his glasses back on. "That Karl. He stood up to his Father. He went against his will. What courage, that Karl."

When we wearily climbed the stairs, Father first, then Mama, then me, I looked back at the neglected presents lying under the tree. No matter, this year. All I could think of as I crawled into bed was Karl. Scenes from those frightening photographs in the papers flooded my mind—men on crutches, trying to smile; heads, feet, arms wrapped in bandages, bandages covering blinded eyes, dead bodies on stretchers. Karl?

"That Karl! What courage!" I thought. To go to war, this terrible war, is bad enough. To go against his father's will—to disappoint one's own father terribly and have him bottle his anger in silence—!

"Oh, Karl!" I breathed into the darkness and silence of my little room, "Give me some of your courage. Help me to tell Father about Rudi and the Holy Trinity Catholic Church before he finds out from somebody else."

CHAPTER TWENTY

The Father's Will

AS IT HAPPENED, I waited too long. Father did not greet me when he came home the next day. He had been making his usual daily rounds of townspeople. It was his time to stop by the bank, the post office, greeting everyone, parishioners and non-parishioners alike, asking them, "*Wie geht's*. How goes it? How's the family?"

This day, he walked in the door and I knew he had found out. There was a deep scowl on his face. He didn't even look at me. He went right into the Holy of Holies and shut the door. It could be the war—tragedy hitting some family or the whole town. But now, it had to be—me!

We sat through supper in silence. Mama and I tried to make small talk and it was no use. Father's silence was stronger and heavier than all our chit-chat. I dreaded the moment supper would be over. He ate little and when he put down his fork, pushed back his chair and looked soberly at me, a cold fear rippled through me.

"Emma. I must speak with you," he said.

Mama started to pick up the dishes. I got up to help her.

"No. Leave the dishes, both of you. Mama, you must hear this, too."

Mama sat down and reached for her ever present knitting. I let myself down gingerly on the edge of my chair. Father was quiet for a long time, head bent, hands folded across his knees.

"Emma," he finally said, looking at me, the scowl gone, but a suffering sadness clouding his face.

"Emma, I am gravely disappointed. I always thought—I assumed—we trusted one another."

He searched my face as if he were looking for some sign—a protest—an agreement—anything.

"Oh *ja*, Father. I do! We have! I mean—"

Father kept looking at me—searching—searching.

"How is it then," he finally asked, that you went to Holy Trinity Catholic Church one night without asking or telling me—or Mama? When did you go? Did you sneak out? I can't believe you would do this. Not you. But I heard it in town. In a Catholic owned store. 'What did your daughter think of Holy Trinity, Reverend,' they asked. What could I say? Could I lie? Could I tell them I didn't know anything about it? My own daughter's whereabouts? How could you do this to me—to—to us, Emma?"

The walls of our small living room felt as if they would close around me, suffocating me. The floor was too solid. I wished it would open up and swallow me.

"Oh, Father," I gasped and started to cry, solid tears, coming from the deepest part of me. "I meant to tell you. I really did. Right after Karl came home, but—"

"Tears will not help you now, Emma. I am weeping inside, myself, from disappointment. Why could you not tell me? Ask me? Why did you have to deceive me—us," He finished his speech and looked over at Mama whose eyes held fast to her knitting.

"Oh, Father," I cried through tears that started to flow. I tried desperately to hang on to some courage, remembering the wonder and happiness of the time with Rudi, not wanting my father to spoil it.

Suddenly, without warning, Father stood up, looming over me. "Don't 'oh, Father' me, young lady. What have I ever done to make you afraid of me?"

There it was—the anger he said was there, but I never saw directed at me—until now. The silence was awful. I kept my head down. Not daring to look at my father, I finally whispered, "I am afraid of you, Father."

I was afraid that very moment, but I wouldn't let myself stop. I went on, a little louder, raising my head a little, making myself look at my father. "I'm afraid to go against your will. It's strong, you know. I'm afraid I'll disappoint you. And that's the worse thing of all. How could I ask you if I could go to a Catholic church with a Catholic boy? You wouldn't allow me. Would you? You'd make me feel sinful for even thinking about it."

The anger that flashed out from my father was suddenly gone. The hurt look, the pained, disbelieving cloud of disappointment and betrayal covered his face as he looked at me, wordlessly.

I longed to run to him, to comfort him, to promise I'd never, ever do it again. Then, I remembered Karl's courage and I remembered Rudi and I kept still. This time, for the first time in my life, I broke the silence. "Father," I ventured to ask in a whispery voice, still barely looking at him, "What's wrong with Catholics, anyway?"

Father took out his handkerchief and wiped his eyes. "*Ach*, Emma. It's not the Catholics—not people who are Catholics." He paused, frowning, before he went on. "It's the church—the pope—the idea that they have all the answers. You'd have to raise your children to be Catholic, Emma, if you married one."

"But, Father, I'm not talking about marriage. I'm just going on sixteen."

Mama stirred, but didn't look up from her knitting. "I was seventeen when I married your father," she said. "One thing leads to another."

"But, Mama," I started to protest, then stopped, remembering the kiss.

"Your mother is right, Emma. Better to find a Protestant boy to start keeping company with. A good Methodist boy—like Karl, maybe."

I stood up from my chair, looking down at my father, shocking myself, frightening myself even further, "Who says I'm going to be a Methodist all my life!" I almost shouted. "I can't dance, I can't play cards. I have to make my feelings go a certain way!"

Silence. Mama dropped her knitting and looked at me with her mouth open. Stunned surprise in Father's eyes slowly deepened further into hurt and reproach.

"Is this our Emma?" he said, softly, sorrowfully.

I was beginning to feel like the cruelest person on earth, but still, I went on. "Really, Father. What about being an instrument of peace, like Saint Francis said? He was Catholic, you know!"

I watched Father's shoulders droop, his face crumple, but I couldn't seem to stop. "I don't know who I am, anymore. I'm tired of being holier than thou. I'm tired of being a German-American Methodist minister's daughter, anti-war, anti-dancing—anti-Catholic! I'm me! Emma Louise Altenberg. Plain American."

After a long silence, it was Mama who recovered.

"Well, I must say," she began, "that's not so bad, I guess. I'm Anna Marie Chersky Altenberg. More than that. Since my parents came from Russia and my mother's parents came to Russia from Germany and my father was Jewish in Russia and then became Lutheran in America, so you could say I am Russian-German-Jewish-Lutheran-Methodist-minister's wife. But I'm still just plain me. Tante to some. Mama Altenberg to many."

I wanted to hug her, but the atmosphere was too tight.

"True, Mama," Father said, his voice full of sorrow. "It doesn't matter what we call ourselves in the long run. I'm proud of being German, and Methodist, even if Emma isn't. It's her deceit that is so painful and disappointing."

He turned away from us both, and shoulders drooping, shuffled into the Holy of Holies, shutting the door behind him.

Mama picked up her knitting again, shaking her head. I started upstairs. I had to work on my essay, like it or not. School was starting Monday and I was supposed to have it finished. I'd have to deal with Father's anger and disappointment and my own sudden outburst alone. The anger I felt was gone. Would I be living with silence from my father all the rest of my born days? The loneliness I felt was heavy, making it hard for me to lift my feet as I climbed the stairs to my room, my own "holy of holies."

CHAPTER TWENTY-ONE

A Brief Encounter

OUR HOME, MY home, had always been a sanctuary for me, more so, even, than church. Now, a chilly silence filled the rooms with things not said, feelings not expressed. Even Mama was strangely silent. I had hurt and angered my father. He had hurt and angered me. Would the wounding ever heal? Could we ever forgive each other? I didn't think I ever could.

I could hardly wait to get back to school, away from this place that now felt like a foreign country to me. I wanted to get back to my friends, the *Graphos* staff, Glee Club practice—Rudi. Especially Rudi. How would he be with me after our mystical time in his church? And after—in the softly falling snow? How would I be with him?

The first Monday after the holiday, my best friends and I met in the hall, shook the snow off our boots, hung up our coats and started talking all at once.

"Oh, did I ever have a grand time New Year's Eve," Vicky bubbled. "I danced with twelve different boys at Turner Hall. Was it ever fun!"

"We got to stay up until midnight," Bertha added. "Max and I had the last dance of 1917 together. It was wonderful, waltzing, cheek to cheek."

"What about you, Emma?" Bertha asked. "What was your New Year's Eve like?"

At that moment, I hated being a minister's daughter more than ever before. After looking forward so much to being back with friends, I suddenly felt sad and lonely. I longed to belong somewhere—to be a modern, free-thinking Turner—or—a Catholic.

"Well, we have this Watch Night at church, you know—"

The bell rang for classes, saving me from having to pretend excitement about Watch Night at church with oyster stew and after, at home, *rote gröze*, that red fruity sauce with sour cream on top. No boys. No dancing. I longed for Wednesday when I would be meeting Rudi alone after Glee Club practice. Maybe, with him, I could tell all the things that were in my heart. I promised Karl to let Amelia tell about her brother's return and I intended to keep my promise. But maybe I could tell Rudi about the dreadful quarrel with my father. Maybe not, though. It might hurt his feelings—the part about Catholics.

Three days before I could see him alone. Three long days.

It was Rudi himself who shortened the time. He surprised me that very day, in the hall after school. I was putting on my coat when I felt a hand on my shoulder. When I turned around and saw who it was, and saw the soft glow in his eyes, I felt my cheeks grow hot; and yet, I wanted to shout with relief and joy.

"It's good to see you, Emma. I've been wondering how you were. May I walk home with you—part way? I want to talk to you—ask you something."

"*Gern*, Rudi. Gladly! Of course. I'd like you to walk part way with me."

I did not feel alone any longer. With Rudi walking beside me, taking my elbow as we crossed the street, I felt safe, as if we were in a little world all our own.

"There's going to be a dance in our guild hall, Emma. A Valentine's dance. We're raising money to build a Catholic High School as soon as the war is over. Will you come with? Can you? There's going to be lotto and keno and other games. Could you be my partner?"

The walls of the safe world that had enclosed Rudi and me a moment before, crumbled in one, dreadful moment and I felt exposed to another. This world was dangerous, exciting, forbidden. There would be dancing and gambling, and smoking, even. There were no words in me to describe my turmoil.

"Well, maybe you don't care to come, Emma. Maybe—? Did I hurt your feelings the other night? I mean—"

"Oh Rudi—really! Of course not. You must know. It's not that at all. Really! It's—I'd love it, Rudi, more than anything in the world, but I—it's my father, you see."

The crestfallen look on Rudi's face was like a cloud passing over the sun. And I had caused it. Now I had hurt them both—my father and Rudi, both so dear to me—until lately, that is. My father—.

"It's because I'm Catholic, Emma, isn't it?

"I hate it, Rudi, I really do. I sometimes wish I were not my father's daughter—not a Methodist."

"Sometimes I wish I weren't a Catholic, but that's a mortal sin. And it would break my mother's heart if she knew how I felt. I couldn't be anything else but Catholic. I just wish everybody could get along."

We reached the corner where we had to go in different directions. Rudi needed to go on toward Goosetown to his home. I needed to go on toward mine.

"Good-by, Rudi. I'm so sorry."

"Good-by, Emma. I'm sorry, too."

I couldn't bear to watch him walk away, so I turned from him, clutching my books and hugging them to me, wishing it were Rudi I was holding close for comfort. What would there be for me at home or at school in the long, dismal days ahead? What would there be but silence?

CHAPTER TWENTY-TWO

A New Encounter

HER NAME WAS Celestine Armitage and she was the most elegant lady I had seen in my entire life, including Rosa Becker. She was tall, with a regal beauty unlike anyone in all of New Ulm, or the Twin Cities, for that matter. And her voice was liquid music! She stood beside Miss Fletcher in history class the second Monday after the Christmas holiday, and in her presence, I felt like an honored subject before a queen.

I'd heard about her the first moment we girls clustered in the hall between classes.

"You should see her," Katrin said. "She looks like a movie star."

"What's she here for?" Victoria asked, less than impressed.

"Something about patriotism," Bertha added. "A contest or something."

By the time for history class, the last class of the day, I had forgotten all about Miss Armitage. Maybe that was why her elegant presence in our simple, orderly classroom came as such a shock.

"Class, I would like you to meet someone who is graciously giving of her time to New Ulm High School," Miss Fletcher began. Her manner was so much more formal than I had seen in her before this day. She wasn't as exciting a teacher as Mr. Klemm, but was easy with us, not much older than some of us, fresh out of college. Now, her easiness was gone.

"Without further ado, I will let this lovely lady tell you about herself and why she has come to be with us. Class, may I present Miss Celestine Armitage?"

There was a faint murmur and rustling from us and Miss Armitage raised one of her graceful hands to silence us. She held her head as if she were wearing a crown and walked around Miss Fletcher's desk, leaving Miss Fletcher looking like one of us—small, young, inexperienced.

"Ladies and gentlemen," Miss Armitage's voice sounded like a silver bell. "I am privileged to be here. I have heard a great many superlative things about the exceptional talent and intelligence of the students here in this school. That is why you have been chosen to initiate a program of patriotism, which this country so sorely needs."

She paused and smiled at us, revealing beautiful, white, even teeth. She wore a faint tinge of lip rouge, and I thought, or imagined, her breath carried a hint of sweet peppermint. Her bosoms, pushed against her blue satin blouse, were gently rounded. Without thinking, I lifted my hand to cover my flat chest.

"First of all," she continued, "we're counting on you to inspire your parents, friends, relatives, townspeople, to honor our country and our magnificent war effort by promoting the flying of our flag. It is a symbol of all we are and stand for as a nation and we would like to see to it that it flies proudly over all business buildings, in front of every home and in every church in this city. Talk it up. Visit homes, businesses—churches. Let me know how you are doing. I will praise you to the governor and the Minnesota Commission for Public Safety. What an honor to your town. No one can resist the enthusiasm of bright, talented young people."

She laughed lightly, and the rustling and shifting sound coming from us was slightly stronger than before she began. She raised her elegant hand again for our complete attention and then dropped her next words into the silent room as if they were precious pearls.

"Secondly—and this is the most exciting thing! We are initiating an essay contest—the winner of which—will be given—a full year's scholarship to the English-speaking college of your choice—tuition, books, room and board—everything!"

Her voice, her beauty, her carriage riveted me and I couldn't take my eyes off of her as she reached around Miss Fletcher's desk for a piece of paper.

"Now, I would like to get to know each one of you personally. When I call your name, will you please raise your hand so I can greet you and be able to recognize you quickly. I am here to help you with your essays, both the content and the delivery. The winner may even deliver the essay over the radio—to the entire state. What a reputation New Ulm will have!"

"Altenberg. Emma Louise?"

Of course, I was first, and when I raised my hand, she smiled at me warmly and I felt as if I had been anointed. Victoria and Rosa Becker's elegance faded compared to Miss Armitage. Those two, not my own mother, had always seemed to look and be what I longed to become. Now Celestine Armitage glowed like a beacon lighting the way to feminine adulthood for me. I would write the best essay I could, "Why I Am Proud To Be An American," and I might, just might, win the scholarship and Father would be proud of me again. I left the classroom in a daze.

"Well, what do you think?" Victoria asked me on the way home.

"I think she is absolutely the most elegant, wonderful person I could imagine, don't you?"

"Emma Louise Altenberg, I can't believe you. Taken in by that— that—. She's phony, Em! And what an insult to our town. Just like the governor's parade. What do they think we are, up there in Saint Paul, a bunch of dummies—unpatriotic dummies?"

I looked at Victoria with surprise. Could there be a bit of the green-eyed monster in Vicky's opinion of Miss Armitage?

"Well, I think it's swell that we could maybe have a chance to win a scholarship, don't you?" I offered, not wanting to start an argument

"I guess so." Victoria said tucking her chin down into her coat collar.

We walked on without talking or even saying good-bye. I knew that we'd had disagreements before and would get over this one, too.

Still, I couldn't shake the image of elegant Miss Armitage from my mind, but I couldn't forget Victoria's face either. What I had seen in Vicky's eyes did not look like jealousy but sadness. Her father, of course. She's worried about him and even though he had not been suspected of being a spy, the cloud of suspicion that hung over many Turners must be hard for them all. How could I have forgotten? Maybe the presence of Miss Armitage and all her flag waving would seem like a painful insult to Joseph Becker. And my own father. How could I possibly urge him to fly the flag. We were barely speaking. It would be much easier to mend things with Vicky than with Father. Truly.

A week of deep winter went by. We got up in the dark and came home after school in the dark, took hours bundling and unbundling our winter clothes for our walk to and from school. Most of the few country students stayed in town during the week. The roads were too snow filled to bring them in by car, or by sleigh. The Beckers took four students in their large house. Amelia stayed with us in our spare bedroom. It was good having her with us, the sister I never had. She brought some warmth into our house that was chilly these days in more ways than one.

At the end of the week, just after she finished her daily talk about the war effort and patriotism, Miss Armitage called out, "Emma Altenberg, may I see you after class?"

My heart skipped a beat with a mixture of apprehension and excitement. When the rest of my class had filed out of the room, Miss Fletcher picked up her books, waved at me and left me alone with Celestine Armitage.

"Emma," she began, plunging right in, tilting her head and smiling her beguiling smile, "I understand that you are a fine writer, but I haven't received your essay—yet. Mr. Klemm gave you this assignment before he went away last spring. If you are having trouble with it, perhaps I can be of help?"

"I'm sorry, Miss Armitage—truly. I—it's just that I've thought about it so much and I just can't seem to get it right."

"I appreciate your conscientiousness, Emma. So, I have a thought, and I'm wondering if you would be interested?"

"*Ja?*" I asked.

"Oh, dear me, Emma. Everyone in New Ulm seems to say *Ja*," and she laughed her silver-toned laugh. "How about 'yes'—or better yet, 'yes, ma'am.' That response indicates a sense of culture and refinement in our country."

"I'm sorry, Miss Armitage. Yes, ma'am."

"Thank you, Emma. That's better. Now. The thought I had was this. I really don't have the time here at school, with all the classes I have to visit. So I was wondering if there would be any chance at all of your coming to the cities, with your father, perhaps, when he goes to those meetings in Saint Paul. We could work on your essay, both the content and delivery in the privacy of my home. I think you might have a good chance of winning this contest."

My skin started to prickle. What was my sudden discomfort all about? And how did she know about Father's meetings in Saint Paul? But this was the magical Miss Armitage. In spite of Vicky's disapproval of her, she was remarkable and sent out by the governor to help us.

"Well, Miss Armitage, ma'am. I can ask Father. We have gone with him, my mother and I sometimes, but lately —"

"Lately?" Miss Armitage smiled an encouraging smile.

"Well, lately, he has to go by train, you see. In the winter, that is."

"Oh, yes, of course. Well, perhaps you'd like me to visit you and have me ask your father?"

"Oh no! I mean, he's really so busy. No, no, ma'am. I'll ask him. Thank you, but no! It won't be necessary for you to take that time." Father and Miss Armitage? The thought made me quiver.

I picked up my books and hugged them to me, eager to leave. "Oh—and thank you, Miss Armitage!"

"It's my privilege, Emma. I'm happy to be of help to all of you in New Ulm—for our great country."

I turned to leave the room. Her voice stopped me.

"Oh, and Emma. Before I forget. Have you talked to your father about flying the flag in your church? I understand yours is one of the churches in town that has not yet done this. It's so important, Emma. Our flag is a beacon. A rallying point for us all."

"I'll try, Miss Armitage. He's been so busy lately."

"I'm sure he has. But do try, Emma. Let me know how you get along. Your father is such an important and influential man in this town. He could be such a fine example. But, run along, my dear. I'm sorry I've kept you so long."

"*Wieder*—I mean, good-day, Miss Armitage."

Rudi had not waited to walk home with me. Basketball practice, of course. Still, there was the sinking feeling inside me that our last conversation had hurt him too much and our relationship might be coming to an end. I thought I couldn't bear it. Victoria hadn't waited for me, either, and Amelia apparently went home to study or help Mama. I pulled my scarf up over my mouth and my nose and walked on home alone, too numb with cold and confusion to think.

At home, Amelia's quiet presence eased the tension between Father and me and made it natural to talk about things that were happening at school, especially the presence of Miss Armitage. Amelia brought up the subject herself. I didn't have to, thank goodness.

"She's beautiful—has a beautiful voice—but—"

"But what, Amelia?" Mama asked, straight out.

"Well, I don't know, really. It's just that she's so patriotic. Seems like I don't have a chance to have my own feelings. You know? And the flag. All the talk about it." Tears were filling Amelia's yes.

Mama reached over and covered Amelia's hand with her own. Father frowned. I wanted to cry, too. The painful memory of Onkel Dietrich's humiliation was like an ugly presence among us.

"I will not fly the flag in my church," Father announced firmly. "The church is a sanctuary, dedicated to Christian ideals. Our constitution guarantees separation of church and state. The flag doesn't belong there. It's a symbol of government—not religion!"

"But Father—," I started to protest.

Mama jumped up from the table. "Canned peaches and coffee, everyone? I think we've had enough seriousness for a while."

"You were going to say, Emma, before dessert," Father asked as Mama and Amelia got up to clear the table for coffee and peaches.

"Well, I was going to say, I think Miss Armitage means well. She thinks she's doing her patriotic duty. And the contest. Don't you think that's wonderful?"

Father looked at me a long time before he answered, his frown deepening. "I'm not sure, Emma. If you young people write sincerely, perhaps. But just to write high sounding words to win a contest? I disapprove."

The father I had known seemed to be totally gone, gone from this room, gone from my heart. How could I ever ask him about Miss Armitage's offer. How could I go on a trip to the Cities with him?

We ate canned peaches and drank coffee and talked about the weather a little. But after Father's outburst, the easiness was gone, and we fell into an uncomfortable silence.

The telephone call came just as we were about to leave the table. Father answered it and when he came back to the table he sat down without looking at me.

"It was your Miss Armitage, Emma. She told me she had offered to help you with your essay next time I go to Saint Paul. She wondered if a time could be arranged. I'm going Saturday. You may come along. I need to meet your Miss Armitage."

He looked at me then, the sorrow in his eyes I knew so well, "I must say, Emma, it grieves me deeply you could not tell me about this yourself."

"I—I—," I stammered.

Before I could think of anything else to say, Father went on, searching my face as he spoke, "You don't need to say anything, Emma," he said. "You don't need to remind me you are afraid to be honest with me."

He got up, left the table, and disappeared into his study, leaving me with no time for a reply. There was nothing left for me to do but join Mama and Amelia for dishes in the kitchen, which I did with a heavy heart.

CHAPTER TWENTY-THREE

The Universal Language

THE CABOOSE OF the Union and Pacific freight train was the only one we could catch before noon for the trip to Saint Paul. As soon as we seated ourselves on the benches opposite one another, Father put his briefcase on his lap and used it as a writing table. He told me he needed to make notes of some of the points he wanted to make to the Bishop and fellow ministers about dissolving the German Methodist Church and joining the Methodist Episcopals. We rattled through the frozen countryside in silence. I might as well not have been there.

My uneasiness about my father and Celestine Armitage meeting one another grew with every passing mile. Father still had a thick German accent, often using German words if he couldn't think of a better English one. He couldn't keep his opinions to himself. What would Miss Armitage think of him? And Father. Would he be as charmed as I was by her elegant ways, her silvery voice? An uncomfortable, sinking feeling swept through me the nearer we got to Saint Paul.

She met us at the door, all smiles, and held out her hand. "I'm delighted, Reverend Altenberg," she said. "I've heard so much about you. Do come in."

"Charmed," Father answered, taking her hand and bowing in his courtly way. "*Es freut mich*. I am pleased."

Inward, I winced. Didn't Father remember that it was *verboten*, forbidden, to speak German? Or was he doing this on purpose? Couldn't he be more careful—just this once?

Miss Armitage raised her eyebrows, but held the door open for us as we walked in. There was a warm fire crackling in the fireplace at one end of the living room and a grand piano with a Spanish shawl draped over it at the other.

"Ah, a grand piano!" Father said. "*Wunderbar!* Wonderful! You play, Miss Armitage?"

"Oh my, yes. Yes, indeed. I've studied piano and voice for many years and before the war I had plans to become an opera singer."

What a perfect beginning, I thought, my doubts melting away in the warmth of a mutual love—music, the universal language, Father had often said.

"Ah! Can you believe it? Would you be willing, *Fraulein*, gracious lady, to sing for us? I have a bit of time and we would be so honored."

I couldn't tell for certain how Miss Armitage was taking Father's accent, his frequent use of German words and phrases; but she smiled, revealing her beautiful teeth.

"Reverend Altenberg, how kind of you to ask. I don't get enough opportunity to perform these days—the war, you understand. What would you like to hear? How about 'My Heart At Thy Sweet Voice' from *Samson and Delilah*—a Biblical opera. You might like that?"

"*Gut!* Excellent!" Father said.

Something was going on between these two that I didn't really understand. Just as on the train, I felt as if I might as well not have been there. But I watched intently as Miss Armitage adjusted her skirt, sat down on the piano bench, lifted her graceful hands above the keys and began to sing, accompanying herself skillfully.

It was truly beautiful and Father applauded when she had finished, took out his handkerchief and lifted his glasses to wipe the tears from his eyes.

"You are an artist, Miss Armitage," he said.

"Thank you, thank you, Reverend. And now, how about you. I understand you have a fine voice. Would you sing for me?"

"Well, now," Father demurred. "I don't have any music with me, but—"

He looked at me, and raised his eye-brows. "Perhaps Emma can remember something by heart, and accompany me."

Father loved to perform, that had always been clear to me, but this was supposed to be my time with Miss Armitage. I shook my head no.

"*Ach, ja*, Emma. How about "*Die Uhr?*"—The Clock. I think you can remember that. You've played it so often for me."

Father straightened his shoulders and walked to the piano, gesturing in a grand manner for me to sit at the piano.

I obeyed, against my will and played the introduction, fumbling just a little. Father began to sing in his resonant bass voice the German words to "The Clock."

He had not finished the first phrase when Miss Armitage stood up from her chair and broke in. "Oh, no, Reverend. Please! No! Not in German. Can't you sing it in English? Don't you know the words in English?"

The look on Father's face was one I knew well. Hurt. As though he had been struck. He stood silently for a moment. Then, he squared his shoulders and turned to me, away from Miss Armitage. "Thank you, Emma, that will be all. I do not know the words in English. I haven't translated them. They are beautiful enough in German."

"It seems to me, Reverend," Miss Armitage said, the smile gone from her face, "that this is America, an English-speaking country, and you would do well to use it. I sang an Italian song in English, you may have noticed."

There was a chill in her voice that I had never noticed. The magical bond of the universal language of music was broken. They should have sung songs without words, I thought, just la, la, la. The chilly moment did not last long, because Father asked for his coat and started to leave.

"You can catch the street car, Emma, to the German Methodist headquarters. Meet me there. About four o'clock. You have the directions. We must catch the six o'clock train. *Guten tag*. Good day, Miss Armitage."

He put his favorite clipped beaver hat squarely on top of his head and left.

"Ah, my dear," Miss Armitage said, as she closed the door after Father. She put her arm around my shoulder and led me back into the living room. "How embarrassing for you. I'm so sorry. But your father seems so reluctant to let go his German ways. How do you account for that? He seems such a fine man. It's so sad he can't embrace his American way of life. Don't you agree?"

"I—well, you see—"

"Emma, my dear, come sit down. Let's talk about this. Maybe this is why you're having so much trouble with your essay? Could that be?"

"I—I'm not sure, Miss Armitage. That is—"

"Well, now, it's abundantly clear you are a very intelligent young lady, mature beyond your years. Surely you must have some feelings, some opinions about why your father clings to his German sympathies so—so stubbornly?

"Germans are noted for their stubbornness, you know," she added with a little laugh.

"I hadn't thought of my father as stubborn, but—"

"But what? What is the doubt in your mind? I see it, my dear. I see it in your face. There's something troubling you about your father, isn't there?"

How could I possibly tell Miss Armitage about my argument with Father, about Rudi, about Catholics, about hyphenated Americans? Especially, how could I tell her about the rumors Rudi told me that some people suspected that Father was a spy?

"He is a Christian minister, Miss Armitage. He really believes in peace on earth."

"But, my dear. We are at war. With Germany. Many, many ministers—most ministers throughout the country—believe it is their Christian duty to fight the German barbarians with everything in our power. Peace is an ideal we all strive for, of course. But bayoneting babies, raising armies to conquer the world! That must be stopped—by whatever means—with all our force!"

I found myself sitting on the edge of the chair as she talked, my fingers gripping the velvet seat cushion. I tried to keep calm. She must
not guess the turmoil inside me.

Miss Armitage pulled up a chair, sat down beside me and went on.
"Listen to me! You're old enough, now, to do your own thinking. Your
father may not always be right about everything, you know. We often
think of our fathers as gods—when we're very young—before we're
old enough to do our own thinking."

Where had I heard that before? Vicky! What would Vicky say if she
were here?

"You are in a most difficult position, I know," she said, her voice full
of sympathy. "Believe me, when I say you can trust me. I will help you
with your essay. You must think carefully about why you really are
proud to be American. Emma, you believe in democracy, don't you?"

"Oh, yes, I certainly do."

"And you believe we must do all we can to preserve it in the world?"

"Why, yes. Yes, I do."

"Would you be willing to do something, right now, to help your
country—to save the world for democracy?'

"If I can. If it's—well, not unconstitutional," I managed to say.

"Oh, my dear, you are wonderful. All that has been said about you
is true. Of course, I wouldn't ask you to do anything unconstitutional.
But, Emma, you can help your country so much—by keeping your
eyes and ears open, being alert to anything, coming from anywhere
that might be disloyal to our country, sound subversive or treason-
able. You understand?"

"I'm not sure I do. I think I do. I guess."

"Of course you do. It may all seem perfectly innocent to you, but it's
like the parade and the rally New Ulm had in July. They thought, the
leaders did, that they were innocent. But, Emma, they were not! They
were doing something totally disloyal!"

"But Dr. Fritsche, Pfaender, Vogel are so—"

Miss Armitage stood up, erect, towering over me. "Don't talk to me about Fritsche or Vogel or Pfaender or Steinhauser or Ackermann or Becker or any of the rest of them. Please."

She started pacing again as she went on, her voice rising. "Those men made themselves pawns to subversion. They undermined the confidence of your entire town in itself. They brought down scorn and derision. Everyone in the whole United States suspects New Ulm of treason! And it's justified!"

She stopped her pacing and stood in front of me, looking down at me. "Emma Louise, I'm asking you, right out—was your father,—is your father, one of them? You must know. You live right there in his house. You must have heard things. Did those men receive directions from somewhere else?"

I stood up, too. "Miss Armitage. I'm sorry. But may I use your bathroom?"

"Ah, my dear," Miss Armitage answered, quickly recovering her lost poise. "Of course. How thoughtless."

When I came out of the bathroom, Miss Armitage had calmed down completely. She smiled her warm smile and laughed her bright little laugh.

"You must excuse my fervor," Emma. "I'm so in love with my country that I'd do anything for it. I'm so concerned some of us may unwittingly aid and abet our enemy. Do you understand?"

Everyone was asking me to understand these days. I was having a hard time understanding any of it. Why weren't we working on my essay? Why the patriotic speeches. Why was I feeling so strongly I wanted to leave?

"I guess my time is about over, Miss Armitage. I mustn't miss the street car."

"Oh, my," she said, "I'm so sorry. We didn't get around to working on your essay, did we? Not one single minute. I guess I did get a bit carried away."

She sounded so genuine, I almost forgot my uneasiness.

"And you have to meet your father, don't you, at the German

Methodist headquarters? Do you happen to know, Emma, what the meetings are all about?"

"Not much, really," I said.

"Well, I couldn't help wondering, some of us have been wondering, if the German Methodist Church in America had any connection with the Methodist Church in Germany? And could there be any correspondence between them? Do you think?"

"I don't think so, but—"

"But you're not sure?"

"I haven't been to any of the meetings, naturally. I haven't read any correspondence, either."

I chose not to tell her about Father's whispered conversations behind the closed doors of the Holy of Holies. I didn't tell her about the increasing numbers of calls and meetings in Saint Paul. I chose not to tell her anything, the beautiful Miss Armitage.

"Well, naturally. But, if you do—Oh dear me, you need to go, don't you? I'll get your coat."

As I put on my coat, eager to leave, to get on the street car and be alone to think, Miss Armitage finished what she started to say.

"One more thing, Emma, before you leave. Remember, how innocent we think we are sometimes. We naively become tools for people with less innocent intent. I want you to do one thing for me. For your country. Keep your eyes and ears open. If you hear anything, anything that troubles you, let me know, would you? You surely can trust me."

"Thank you, Miss Armitage. I'll remember. And thank you for wanting to help me with my essay."

"You're more than welcome, my dear. I am sorry we didn't get around to your essay. Another time, hopefully."

She closed the door. I walked down the steps and hurried to catch the street car that would take me to the German Methodist Church headquarters on the other side of town.

CHAPTER TWENTY-FOUR

The Man In The Brown Coat

IT WAS SIX blocks from Miss Armitage's house to the street corner where I caught the street car. Father had given me instructions and I didn't think I'd be afraid. I met a few people coming as I walked along and we nodded at one another. One or two were going in my direction and passed by me from behind. People in the city walked so fast.

I was certainly in no hurry. I had been in a hurry to leave Miss Armitage's, but now I would have to find a way to use the time, before Father would be expecting me. Even though it was too cold for a stroll, I could walk briskly up and down the streets and enjoy the neighborhood to use up some time.

There were large, beautiful houses set back from the side walk on both sides of the street. Black, empty branches of great elm trees arched over my head, clutching at the swiftly darkening sky. Soon I felt like I was walking in an unreal, dangerous world.

I had gone about three blocks when I became aware of a man in back of me who did not catch up to me and seemed to measure his steps to stay behind me. He wore a plain brown coat. I shivered and pulled the collar of my coat up around my ears. The uneasiness I began to feel at Miss Armitage's made my imagination run away with me. "Keep your eyes and ear open," Miss Armitage had said and Rudi's warning came back to me, full force, "There are spies. Warn your father—some people think he may be a spy."

As I turned corners of the dark streets, hoping to lose the man, I thought I felt his presence still behind me. Had he been sent by someone to follow me? I hadn't seen him when I first left Miss Armitage's. How could he tell I was me, daughter of a man some thought to be a spy? Could he tell I was a German-American from New Ulm? Was it

135

my clothes? My walk? Would he catch up with me to question me? I began to panic and started to run. I knew that was the wrong thing to do, like giving myself away, but I couldn't help it. I had to get away. I had to get to the lighted corner where I was to pick up the street car. I didn't dare turn around to see if I was still being followed.

When I got to the lighted corner, there was no one there—not even the man in the brown coat. But as I stood there, out of breath, still shaking, a few people began to arrive and I felt a little safer.

It wasn't long before the street car arrived, screeched to a stop and my turn to climb aboard finally came. When I got on, I asked for a transfer and looked behind me to see if the brown coated man was there. He was. And he asked for a transfer, too. My panic returned. He sat down a few seats in front of me, so all I could see of him was the back of his head. He looked like an ordinary, everyday man on his way home from work.

Even if he were a spy, what could he do to me in a public place like this street car? Still, I suddenly felt all alone. I thought of Mama, I thought of school and Victoria and Rudi and pretended they were here beside me as we clanged and rattled along.

Brown coat transferred at the same place I did, caught the same new street car, sat in the seat opposite me. What if he leaned across the aisle and tried to start a conversation with me? Would he notice my New Ulm accent? I held my breath. But he opened a newspaper, hiding his face and I breathed again.

As we rode along, I wondered if I should ride past the headquarters of the German Methodist Church, to throw the man off, but decided I was being hysterical, so I got off at the right corner and the man rode on. My relief was so great, I wanted to cry.

Father was waiting for me. He seemed to be in a grave mood. The meeting was over, but he introduced me to the Bishop and some other men, and we said good-bye in English and left. We had to catch the street car quickly to take us to the train station for our journey home.

On the way back to New Ulm, we took a passenger train and sat next to one another. We just settled into our seats when I thought I saw the same Brown Coat come down the aisle and sit a few seats in front of us. There are lots of brown coats in this world. I couldn't be absolutely certain this was the same one, but when Father started talking to me in an ordinary voice, I put my hand on his knee.

"What's the matter? *Was ist los*, Emma?" he said aloud. "Is it your Miss Armitage? You're disappointed I didn't take to her?"

I lowered my head and mumbled, "I think we're being followed."

"Nonsense," he answered, but dropped his voice.

Our conversation all the way back to New Ulm was about the cold weather, the growth of Saint Paul, the longing for spring. Mostly, we were silent. The man got off at the station in New Ulm close behind us and walked in the direction of town, carrying a brief case. We walked on home in the dark winter night.

"Let's not tell Mama about the man on the train, Emma. She'll worry more than she does already. He was probably just a business man, anyway."

"Good, Father, I agree."

Mama had hot soup waiting for us. She didn't ask anything about the meeting and Father didn't offer any information. Mama didn't ask about the meeting with Miss Armitage, either. She was full of her own experience of this long day.

"You know what that Red Cross lady asked us to do today? Eat carp from the river! She said it's our patriotic duty to save meat. For the war effort, you know. She said we can fish through the ice. And she showed us a fancy way of seasoning the miserable bottom feeders and serving it on a wooden plank, as if we didn't know anything about cooking. And you know what I almost told her? I almost said, "Very good, very beautiful. When it's baked, I'll take it out of the oven, throw away the fish and eat the plank!' That's what I almost told her!"

We laughed almost gaily as we ate our vegetable soup with spaetzles. An ordinary, comfortable feeling began to return to me. But it didn't erase the panic I felt in the dark streets of Saint Paul. The time had surely come for me to warn my father, to question him if I needed to.

Tomorrow was Sunday, Father's work day. But maybe, after church would be a good time. Part of me backed away from the thought. Partly because I thought I noticed a small thaw between my father and me. But I had to do it, even if it meant freezing up into silence again. I had to do it—for both our sakes.

After church, after Sunday dinner, Father relaxed with the Sunday paper in the living room. I came up to him, sat down on the floor beside his chair, and laid my hand on his knee.

"Father, I need to talk to you," I began, thinking of Karl, praying for his kind of courage.

Father lowered the paper and looked down at me, a surprised look on his face. "*Ja*? *Was ist los*, Emmeline, what's wrong, my little Emma?"

I was grateful he used his affectionate name for me, even if I didn't feel little anymore. This was it. Now or never.

"I—I was wondering, Father, if you were worried about the man in the brown coat that I thought was following me?" I blurted out. "Do you think—is it possible—he may have been a spy? Do you think Miss Armitage is a spy? Does she think you—you may be spying? She asked questions about you—you and the German Methodist Church."

My heart was pounding. Father folded his paper carefully and put it down. He looked at me a long time before he spoke. "Emma," he said. "We are at war. Terrible things happen to people during wars—not only to soldiers doing the fighting, but to people in the homeland. They become full of fear. They begin to be suspicious of one another. We mustn't let our fears tear us apart or keep us from feeling grateful for each day."

"But Father—if—"

Father didn't let me finish, but put his hand on my shoulder affectionately. "Emma, please—to answer your question—no, I don't think Miss Armitage was a spy, but I do think she is an overzealous person, believing she is a patriot. And no, I'm not worried about the man you thought was following us. You are letting your fears run away with your reason. I'm going to go on saying what I believe, doing what I believe is right, no matter what people may think about me. That is my way of being patriotic. Please, my daughter, try to do the same."

He patted my shoulder, got up from his chair and disappeared into his study.

I had tried. I was far from satisfied, but I had tried. What more could I do? I thought I'd go up to my room and think about my essay, which I kept postponing. I climbed the stairs to my room, thinking and thinking about what father had said—and did not say.

I took out my tablet, picked up a pencil and wrote, "Why I am Proud To Be An American." That's as far as I got.

CHAPTER TWENTY-FIVE

Alienation

I WAS EAGER to get back to school Monday morning, in spite of my dread of seeing Miss Armitage again. At school, I thought I could get away from the war, the confusion about what Father had said—Miss Armitage's suspicion about the German Methodist Church, and the man in the brown coat. I could get back into the real world, my school and my friends' world of planning for the Prom and graduation exercises, getting excited about the progress of our basketball team, and especially, seeing Rudi. Maybe seeing him would ease my awful fears about so many things. Fear! I hated it!

Thinking about Rudi all day, searching for him in the hall, I almost forgot Miss Armitage. I remembered her just before the last class. I walked into our classroom, trying to look calm.

She was cool, but still beautiful. She looked tired and her beauty seemed brittle this Monday morning, like crystal that would easily shatter if not handled properly. I felt sorry for her, in spite myself, in spite of her suspicious questioning about Father. I didn't agree with Father about her. She may not have been a out and out spy, but she sure seemed like an informer to me. What did she know about Father I didn't know?

"I expect you all to have your essays in by the end of the week," she announced. "Then, after school, I'll start to help some of you with your delivery. Some of you still have an noticeable New Ulm accent, and that will work against you in the contest for the scholarship."

Stephan Schroeder, Victoria's sweetheart, raised his hand.

She looked at him and smiled, but with her mouth closed.

"Yes, Mr. Schroeder?"

"Miss Armitage, our debate team has won the regional contest and we have a state declamatory winner in our school. Being from New Ulm has not gone against us in the past."

Good for him, I thought. Father would approve. Mama, too.

Miss Armitage managed a full smile and raised her graceful hand. "Of course, Mr. Schroeder. But now, we are at war. Having an accent is not a good thing for a patriotism contest. You must realize this, I am sure. It will only take a bit of work to solve the problem. I am sure, also, that you will all do all in your power to do credit to your town, as well as for yourselves, by writing the best essays you are capable of."

A few more hands went up, but Miss Fletcher came from around her desk and stood beside Miss Armitage. "Class, Miss Armitage will only be in our school through this week. This is her last time with us. We can learn much from her in this short remaining time. Let's show our appreciation of her sharing her time and talent with us and give her a hand."

We responded with a smattering of applause and Miss Armitage looked embarrassed. A dark, angry look clouded her beautiful face, but she tried to smile it away.

"Thank you, ladies and gentlemen. It's been a privilege," she said and floated out of the room. And out of our lives, I hoped.

It seemed like Wednesday and Glee Club practice after school would take forever to come. I needed to know more than anything in the world if things had changed between Rudi and me since our last conversation about the Catholic problem. I tried to catch his eyes during rehearsal, but he looked steadfastly at Miss Schmidt, our director. Practice seemed to drag as it never had before and the singing seemed half-hearted.

When the hour was up, I slowly gathered my music, forcing myself not to look to see if Rudi intended to stay for our usual English practice. When Miss Schmidt put down her baton and dismissed the Glee Club, I saw that Rudi had not left the room with the others.

Oh, joy! No matter what he might need to tell me, our last conversation wasn't going to be the last. Miss Schmidt gave us a brief wave and closed the door behind her. We were alone.

"Let's work on my accent, Emma. Miss Armitage says we sound funny. If I go away to school next year, I don't want to sound funny."

We got right to work on Theophilous Thistle, but neither of us laughed at ourselves when we stuck our tongues between our teeth for the "th's." When our time was up, Rudi closed his book with his usual snap. I longed to close the distance that had risen between us by running into his arms for comfort and reassurance. But, of course, I didn't. I couldn't. He'd have to make the first move.

"Emma," he said, looking directly at me, his eyes dark as forest pools, "since we are friends, you know, I wanted to ask you what you'd think if I asked Victoria Becker to the Valentine's dance at our church. Since you can't go, I thought maybe—"

"Oh, my g-g-goodness, Rudi," I stammered. An image of the snowy evening after the Holy Trinity visit suddenly rose up in my mind; only now I saw beautiful Victoria Becker in Rudi's arms. Oh, no!

"Why, Rudi," I said out loud. "Oh, my goodness. Well, of course. I mean, yes, of course. That's a good idea," I lied.

"You would be my first choice, Emma. But—"

"*Ich verstehe,*" I said, slipping into German without realizing it. "I understand. I can't dance."

"And I'm Catholic, Emma. And your father—"

"I don't share my father's views about everything, Rudi. I can do my own thinking, you know."

Where did that come from? Who was I, anyway?

"But you couldn't go against your father, Emma. I know you. It will hurt you too much. I just thought Victoria being your friend it would be all right with you. I wouldn't go at all except I'm expected to."

He would never, ever know how I really felt. Victoria was my best friend, true. But I didn't trust her. How could I tell him that. Didn't he know it was worse that he would ask my best friend? What kind of people are boys, anyway?

But I smiled and said, "Of course, Rudi, it's just fine. Really," feeling as false as ersatz flour. We said good-bye to each other. He didn't offer to walk home with me.

I couldn't wait to get home. I would have run if it hadn't been for the icy sidewalks. For the first time since I was a small child and fell on the ice, cracking my head and getting a small concussion, I wanted my mother! But who else could I talk to? Obviously not Victoria. Certainly not Father. Mama was the only one that just might understand. So many people had run to her arms lately for warmth and comfort. It was my turn now.

A strange man stood in the living room, not the Holy of Holies, talking to Father, who was scowling, looking troubled. The man was not wearing a brown coat, but had an American flag in his coat lapel.

"Emma, your mother's upstairs," Father said, not taking his eyes from the man. "Go to her."

"Well, Reverend, shall we go?" the stranger announced. "The office will be open until six."

"I will come later—on my own," Father said, the look on his face darkening even more.

"I don't think so, Reverend. Get your coat."

There was a long pause, while the two men stared at each other. Then, Father squared his shoulders.

"Very well. As you say," he said.

He didn't look at me, but passed by me without a word, got his coat and left the house with the stranger.

I had been rooted to the spot, but when the door closed behind the men, I tossed my coat on a chair and flew upstairs to Mama. She sat in front of her vanity dresser. When I walked in, she was pulling her long, thick, brown braid around in front of her, fingering it open until it fell in a shimmering cascade in her lap. She picked up her ivory comb and began her daily ritual of combing. She looked at herself in the mirror as she combed, her eyes gleaming with tears.

She saw me in the mirror as I stepped close to her. She gasped a little, turned around to me and buried her face in my skirt.

"Oh, my, Emma. The worst thing," she sobbed.

I thought sure Father was being arrested for being a spy.

"What is it, Mama?" I said, patting her head as if she were the child, and I her mother.

"You won't believe it. But the authorities found out something, even I didn't know."

"Mama?"

"Your father, Emma. He's an alien! He never sought American citizenship! Now he has to go down to the armory and register—as an alien."

"An alien? Father? How can this be?" It never entered my mind my own father wasn't a citizen of this country.

My mother continued, "He told the man he thought he was a citizen. That when his father became a citizen, that made his children citizens, too. Lots of people thought the same thing, but it's not so. Your father was born in Germany. He was fourteen years old when he came to this country. He was supposed to register on his own."

Mama's sobs had quieted, but her tears still flowed. I kept patting her head, visualizing my father being dragged down to the armory to register—as an alien! It was bad enough that Rudi's mother was an alien. But Father? Dignified Father, pastor of the Ger—.

My thoughts stopped. I felt cold. In my head, I heard Miss Armitage ask me, "Is there any connection between the German Methodist Church in America and the Methodist Church in Germany, do you think?"

Mama might guess my thoughts, mind-reader that she was, so I pushed the memory out of my head. She went back to combing her hair, slowly, carefully, as though seeking comfort in this, another of her rituals.

"Emma—he's such a good man, your father. This shouldn't be happening to him. His pride. His confidence. I know you've had trouble with him lately—about Rudi and the Catholic thing. But he means well, Emma —for sure. He's only thinking of your own good. In the long run."

I took the comb gently from Mama's hand, drew her long hair around so that it flowed down her back, sat on the bench beside her, and began slowly combing her hair for her.

"I know, Mama, but—"

"I don't think you do, Emma. Your Father is a special man—to women, Emma. I might as well tell you now. You're old enough. He— he had to teach me everything when we were married. You understand? And then, I lost three babies before you were born. They died inside me. And your father—after that—never—well, he never forced himself upon me. You understand?"

She began crying again. I stopped combing. With her long, dark hair flowing down her back, and tears glimmering in her eyes, she looked to me like a tragic figure in mourning, not the round, feisty Mama I had always known. A surge of tenderness rose up inside me. "And my own father," Mama went on. "He wasn't that way at all. He drank. He drank up all our extra money and was mean when he drank. But your father has never, ever been mean to anyone—not me—not anyone."

We sat on the vanity bench together for a long time. Mama wiped her eyes, deftly rebraided her hair and twisted it into a crown on top of her head. "Well, now," she said, when she had finished. "Let's go down to the kitchen and have some coffee."

Drinking our coffee in this new, woman-to-woman closeness, I told her more about my feelings for Rudi than I had told anyone before. She listened. I went on and on.

"And he's asked me to the Valentine's dance and I can't go because he's Catholic and I can't dance and—and now he's going to ask Victoria Becker. And Mama, I can't stand it!"

Now, it was my turn to cry.

"I don't quite understand the Methodist objection to dancing, Emma. But I think it has something to do with holding each other so close. It leads to other things, you know. And not all boys are kind, like your father. They can get to a point where they're—they're—not kind. You understand?"

"Maybe so. But I know Rudi is kind. I just know it." I said, not telling her everything. Not telling her about the kiss, even though we now seemed more like sisters than mother and daughter. I still couldn't tell anyone about that moment. It was too sacred.

"But what am I going to do about Vicky, Mama? Should I ask her not to accept Rudi's invitation? Either way, if she goes, or if I tell her please not to go, I might lose her friendship."

"Tell her the truth, Emma. Tell her how you really feel. That works best in the long run. Remember: 'Real friendship does not freeze in winter.'"

I got up from the table and went over to Mama, pulled her round body close to me and hugged her tight.

It was a long hug. When I released her, Mama took hold of my arms and looked at me with a mischievous grin.

"Why, Emma," she said, "in the last few months, something has happened to you. Your bosoms have started to bloom. We have to go shopping for a larger blouse."

CHAPTER TWENTY-SIX

Bonds and Promises

FATHER CAME HOME just before supper looking drawn and defeated. He went into his study and closed the door before coming into the kitchen to greet us. Amelia came home a little later. She stayed after school these days working on the school annual. On weekends, Dietrich came and got her in his sleigh. That meant we didn't see very much of her, but I was grateful she was with us. Her quiet presence was soothing.

"We decided we had to put Miss Armitage's picture in the annual," she told us at the supper table. "Hardly anyone really liked her, but we didn't want New Ulm to get an even worse reputation by ignoring her. We're not going to put in anything about the war, though. Just little sketches of soldiers and the flag and reports of the patriotic clubs."

Father, who had been silent so far, spoke up, saying, "Young people can be very perceptive."

"Well, she was pretty nosy, really. Asked everybody a lot of questions about their parent's part in the rally. About the Fritsches and Vogels and Pfaenders. No one would tell her anything. Even Walter told her how much people were hurt—not bitter—but hurt and that some even got sick."

That was a lot of talking for Amelia, but she went on. "She asked me about my father and Karl—and—you," she said looking at Father.

She leaned toward Father and whispered, "Some people even think she was a spy!"

My heart stopped. I looked at Father. He was buttering a piece of bread, drawing his knife back and forth. He said nothing. Mama was the only one who responded.

"What is the world coming to?"

We had almost finished supper before Father said anything. He pushed himself up from the table and straightened his shoulders.

"I've decided to try and sell Liberty Bonds."

"Why, Christian!" Mama said, half question, half exclamation.

"*Ja*," Father answered. "*So geht's.* So it goes."

He left the table and we hadn't heard one word about alien registration.

Amelia and I walked to school together the next morning, heads bent against the sharp winter wind. We pulled our scarves over our mouths and noses and our stocking caps down over our foreheads. It was no time to talk.

But when we got to school and unbundled with the rest of the girls, we all started jabbering at once, in low voices.

"Have you heard from Karl," Katrin asked Amelia.

"Oh, *ja*, he's being shipped out already."

"Mr. Klemm is already in France. Maybe they'll meet."

"Are we losing the war?"

"Sh—sh—don't say that. Nothing discouraging. That's not patriotic."

"Someone said they read in a newspaper that we should have been hung along with the Indians in Mankato."

"We read in the paper this morning that a German church in Saint Paul had been burned—to the ground. No people killed—but still —"

"Sh—sh—don't talk about that!"

"Why is this happening to us?"

"Because we're German. German-American. All lumped together, don't you know."

We changed the subject quickly when Mr. Klingman came down the hall, back to our favorite subjects, basketball scores and spring concerts, and—boys.

Victoria met me in the hall between classes, bubbling with excitement. How quickly her moods changed from gloom to joy. Like Mama. I envied them both.

"Guess what, Emma. I'm going to the prom with Stephan Schroeder. He's already asked me and it's months away. I think I'm in love with him, Em. I keep thinking of him all the time and wishing he'd kiss me. I mean, a real kiss, so I could tell for sure. Not one of those eighty-three little pecks. You understand?"

I couldn't tell her how much I understood—from my own experience. That was still my own best-kept secret. And I couldn't just ask her the question that burned in my mind, did Rudi ask her to the Valentine Dance? I reached over and squeezed her hand. "I think I understand, Vicky. And I'm glad about you and Stephan."

She seemed to be too caught up in her own excitement to notice the dullness in my voice.

It was a snow-melting day in late March that the news came to us. During the *Graphos* meeting, Walter spread the *New Ulm Journal* out on the table and we all bent over it and read the sobering headline:

CAPTAIN ARTHUR KLEMM KILLED IN ACTION

Captain Arthur Klemm, beloved teacher of American history at New Ulm High School has been reported killed in action near the city of Paris, France. He will be posthumously awarded a purple heart for singular courage in rescuing five of his wounded men and carrying them to safety. Captain Klemm was one of the first New Ulmites to enlist and was quickly promoted to the rank of Captain. There will be a memorial service at Our Savior's Lutheran church, Saturday at one P.M. and a special service for the students and faculty this Friday at four-thirty P.M.

We huddled together, reading and re-reading the shocking news in silence. Mr. Klingman came in and told us Captain Klemm's body would not be returned to New Ulm, but would be interred in Arlington Cemetery. What a sad insult, I thought. Not one of us spoke.

The atmosphere at school in the days that followed was somber. The flag that had been raised every morning in a special ceremony now flew at half-mast. We set up a table at one end of the gym with pictures of Mr. Klemm and everyone filed past and placed a branch of pine or balsam in front of the pictures. No roses were to be had in all of New Ulm. Father reminded me that evergreens were a symbol of everlasting life for the Germans. I cried myself to sleep that night, thinking of Mr. Klemm, thinking of Karl, thinking of Father with strange, mixed feelings.

It was hard to concentrate on our studies in the weeks that followed Mr. Klemm's death and hardest of all to concentrate on my lessons with Rudi after Glee Club practice. We gave only a few minutes to our lessons. The heart, the eagerness, was gone. Rudi didn't ever touch me, even lightly. We never laughed. Mr. Klemm's death affected Rudi deeply, I knew, but he never talked about it until several weeks after our memorial service.

He closed his book slowly and looked at me soberly.

"How are we going to find out about my brother, Emma?" he asked. "If he's changed his name to Meyers and lied about his family, how is anyone going to know he is really Winfried Meyerdorf? Mother is out of the hospital now, but worried to death. So am I."

"I'm so sorry, Rudi. Maybe your priest will help you."

"Of course, I'll ask him. But it means so much talking to you, Emma. You're the only one I can really talk to like this. The only one that has seen my mother in her spell. Or knows my brother got so angry he hit my mother. You're the only one. I couldn't ask anyone else to go to the Valentine's dance, you must know. I went. But I didn't dance. I didn't feel like it."

"Thank you, Rudi."

We walked home together in silence. We had almost reached the corner where we usually parted. We stopped and looked long and deeply at each other, holding hands. How much I wanted to say to him, as I had to Karl, "I love you, Rudi." But with Rudi, it was different. I couldn't be the one to say it first.

"I am your friend, Rudi. I always want to be."

"That's more important than being Catholic or Protestant, isn't it, Emma?"

"Oh, yes, Rudi. It is."

"Next year, I'll be gone. I'm applying for a scholarship to the school of music in Minneapolis. Father Lempke is helping me. If Winfried—Larry—comes back from the war whole, to look after my mother, I'll be able to go. So I was wondering if you, if your father, I mean, would consider letting me take you to the Prom. This one time? They'll be games in the classrooms for those who can't dance. And it will be in the gym at school and not in our church."

"Rudi, I don't know what to say. My father is so worried, so gloomy about so many things these days. But I'll try. I'll really try. Just this one time."

How good it was to see him smile again. I couldn't spoil it by telling him my real concern about my father. He had told me once to warn my father about the spy rumors and never mentioned it again.

In spite of everything, though, I would try to persuade my father to let me go to the Prom as Rudi's partner. If I promised not to dance. Maybe Amelia would help me, if I brought it up at supper. Or even Mama.

"Thank you, Emma. So much. Good-bye. See you tomorrow."

"Good-bye, Rudi."

"I love you," I whispered to myself as I watched his red stocking cap disappearing down the street.

CHAPTER TWENTY-SEVEN

Spies and Lies

THE RIGHT TIME to ask Father didn't come that night. He was late for supper and barely touched his chicken noodle soup with mashed potatoes on top, a usual favorite of his.

"I can't do it," he said as he pushed his soup away and started rubbing his forehead. "I can't sell bonds anymore. I could sell the bonds, you see, people seem to trust me, but I can't fill in the Blue Cards."

"What are the Blue Cards?" Amelia asked.

"They are cards we're required to fill in when we sell. We ask all these questions. How much money do you make? How do you earn it? And if the people don't give a certain percentage of their income for bonds, they are under suspicion! I'm supposed to report them to the authorities. How can I do that if people trust me? I can't. It's against my principles. It's an invasion of privacy. I wouldn't want anyone investigating me! Where has trust gone?"

"Well, I never!" Mama said.

Father was not through. "Now I wish I had done more to protest this war. All that's left for me is to do all I can to bring it to a speedy conclusion and work for a just peace."

It had been a long time since Father said so much to us. We sat for a moment, not knowing how to respond.

"I'm sorry," Father said when he noticed our silence. "I shouldn't be worrying you with my concerns. Amelia, you have enough to worry about with Karl gone to the war. Excuse me, Mama, Amelia—Emma."

He bowed to us in his courtly way and left the table.

The stillness that followed was awkward. I dared not say one word about my own concern about Father. He didn't want anyone investigating him, he said.

152

I rushed to fill the silence by changing the subject. "Amelia, Vicky and I are going downtown to look at prom dresses Saturday. Do you want to come with us?"

"Thank you, no, Emma. I'm going home. As soon as the roads are dry enough, I'll be staying there during the week. Mama needs me. She worries so much about Karl. But I'll miss you and I do thank you ever so much for letting me stay here this winter."

"We loved having you, Amelia," Mama said.

I got up from the table and hugged Amelia. "It would be fun looking at prom dresses with you and Vicky, even if I won't be going. Like a thing sisters would do. And you're as dear to me as any the sister I could ever have."

"I wish you were going to Prom," Amelia said. "I'll be making my dress. If you were going, we could make ours together."

"That would be nice," I said.

I looked at Mama. She was looking down at her soup, fiddling with her spoon, saying nothing. That was as close as I got to asking about the Prom and going with Rudi. When could I give him my answer? How long would he wait?

"Can you believe it, Em," Vicky bubbled as we strolled along. No use hurrying this sweet spring afternoon. "It's the vernal equinox. Tomorrow it will start to get just a bit lighter each day. Then, April showers. Then—Prom! I'm so excited. Oh, I'm sorry, Em. I forgot. It must be hard, not being able to go with Rudi. If Karl were here, could you—would you?"

"I might. If we didn't dance. But I don't know. I miss Karl, but—"

"Oh, Em, look!"

We were in front of the Bee Hive dry goods store window and there were prom dresses, three of them. One was as glamorous as a movie star's, with a georgette skirt of different lengths and the lowest neckline I'd ever seen. It looked like it just belonged to tall, blond, beautiful Victoria Becker.

"It looks like it has your name on it, Vicky," I said, trying not to sound envious.

"Let's go in and see how much it costs, Em. If it's more than $29.95, I don't think I'll even try it on. Who knows how much longer Pater will be able to practice medicine. I do think of my father, Em. Maybe not as much as you do yours, but still—"

Just at that moment, something caught my eye in the window next door to the Bee Hive. I walked over to get a better look. Vicky followed me. There, in the store window, was a huge sign with an enormous head line. What was spelled out in the paragraphs that followed chilled me to the bones.

SPIES AND LIES

German agents are every where, eager to gather scraps of information about our men, our ships, our munitions. It is still possible to get information through to Germany, where thousands of these fragments—often individually harmless—are patiently pieced together into a whole that spells death to American soldiers and danger to American homes.

The list of 'Do Nots' that followed looked like the Ten Commandments. I clenched my fists as I read and pressed them to my mouth in disbelief.

Do not become a tool of the Hun by passing on malicious, disheartening rumors—gross scandals in the Red Cross—and other tales certain to disturb American patriots and bring anxiety and grief to American parents.

And do not wait until you catch someone putting a bomb under a factory. Report the man who spreads pessimistic stories—cries for peace, or belittles our efforts to win the war.

Send the names of such persons—to the Department of Justice, Washington. Give all the details you can—the fact that you made the report will not become public.

You are in contact with the enemy today, just as truly as if you faced him across No Man's Land. In your hands are two powerful weapons with which to meet him—discretion and vigilance. Use them.

> COMMITTEE ON PUBLIC INFORMATION
> 8 Jackson Place
> Washington, D. C.

Vicky and I stared at each other.

"Is this what that dreadful Celestine Armitage was talking about? What the whole state and the whole nation are thinking about New Ulm? That we are a bunch of spies? My father, your father, our mayor, every German-American alive? How absolutely, totally unfair and ridiculous!" Vicky said, indignation pouring out of her.

No words came to me. Not one. *Report—man who—pessimistic stories—cries for peace—send the names—discretion and vigilance.* These words pounded in my mind.

"Emma? You all right? You look pale!"

I was nauseated, dizzy. It was hard to breathe. Everything seemed unreal.

"Here, Emma," Vicky said, touching my arm. "I think we better go home, I can look at dresses any old day."

Vicky's touch brought me back into the here and now.

"No, I don't want to go home. Let's go to German Park. I've got to talk to you. I've got to tell somebody."

We found a bench in the park and it all poured out—Father's feeling about the flag in the church, his refusal to stop preaching in German, his failure to take out citizenship papers, his protection of Karl Grossbach for so long, his continuing prayers for peace, for America and the enemy, his refusal to fill in the Blue Cards, and especially his trips to the German Methodist headquarters in Saint Paul and his reluctance to drop the German from German Methodist.

When I had run out of possible accusations, Vicky looked at me disbelieving, "Emma, you're not suggesting that your father is a spy?"

"Well—no Vicky, but I'm so torn. Miss Armitage wanted me to find out if there was any connection, any kind of communication between the German Methodist Church here in America and the Methodist Church in Germany. Of course he's not a bomb setting spy, but maybe he is really aiding and abetting the enemy in those ways it said in the spy notices, sending bits and pieces of information, you know. And with Mr. Klemm killed and Karl over there, I couldn't stand it if—"

I couldn't go on. My head was swimming.

"But, Emma—your own father! He's so fair-minded. Pater says he's the most fair-minded person he's ever known. And gentle, too."

"Not always, Vicky. He's not God, you know. You yourself said that. He's prejudiced about Catholics and dancing and he's absolutely fierce about peace."

"What are you going to do, Em? This is awful. The part about the German church connection, especially. Can't you question him? You couldn't possibly report him, could you? Your own father? You may be upset with him now, but—"

"I've tried to question him. But he won't talk. He just says things like people being fearful and suspicious in time of war—and to be grateful—things like that—and then he walks away. I keep wondering if he's hiding something—or if he's afraid I'd spill something—like knowing where Karl was. What would you do, Vicky, if you thought your father were aiding and abetting the enemy, innocently even, like it said in the notice?"

Vicky was quiet for a long time, then, she stood and pulled me up with her. "Come on, Em. Let's go home. I've got to think about this. I can't believe my father—or yours either, would do anything to hurt our country. Pater thinks about the war and all like your father does. But then, he doesn't preach about peace from a pulpit. And the German-Methodist connection? Pater doesn't have that either. That's scary."

A chill rushed through me. I couldn't think of anything to say as we walked slowly along. The thought of father's passing information to his minister friends in Germany, not even quite realizing he might be aiding and abetting the enemy, seemed more real, more possible all the time. He wouldn't mean to hurt our country, but—if he wrote about the rally, and the parade with thousands of enlisted men and the anti-German, anti-New Ulm feelings all around the country— that could certainly be aiding and abetting the enemy. But would it be traitorous, subversive? Would it make him a spy?

"Oh, Vicky," I finally managed to ask, "if you were in my shoes, what would you do?"

"Well, first thing, I'd try to get Pater to tell me what he was doing. But then, if he was doing something questionable, I certainly don't think he'd want me to know—just to protect me. What I didn't know wouldn't hurt me, he'd think."

I thought right away of Miss Armitage and was glad I didn't really know anything—then. Someone, somewhere, may have known some- thing about my very own father I didn't know. Why else would there be suspicions he may be a spy? These frightening thoughts went on inside me even while Vicky was still talking.

"But if your father is sending information to Germany—even if he thinks it's for a good reason—why I don't know what I'd do. But if Pater wouldn't talk—I think I'd have to find a way to get some defi- nite proof, before I confronted him. Not just suspicion. For my own peace of mind I'd have to do it. All this spy stuff going around. It's catching. "

"But if you did find proof and confronted your father and he didn't do anything—"

"Oh, gosh, Emma—I don't know what I'd do. Report him to the authorities? My own father? Someone I really love? All I can say is, I think I'd know what to do when the time came. You will, too," she said, squeezing my arm.

I'd never seen Vicky so bewildered. It comforted me to know how seriously she was taking my dilemma. For once, I took the lead home, making sure we didn't pass by the Spies and Lies poster.

As we walked by the Candy Kitchen where we often stopped for ice cream, I whispered, "What if someone overheard us talking?"

"No one was in there," Vicky said. "And what did we say that was subversive, anyway?"

Spies and lies! Fear, Vicky's mother had said, was catching. We walked home in silence.

CHAPTER TWENTY-EIGHT

The Turning

VICTORIA'S WORDS LINGERED in my mind for days after our meeting, "I'd have to have definite proof," and "You'll know what to do when the right time comes."

I kept wondering how I could find definite proof that my father was aiding and betting the enemy in some way. It was beyond my imagining that he could be an out-and-out—sp—I couldn't even think the word, much less say it to myself. And if I did find out something, what would I do about it? The thought of confronting Father worried me day and night. Would he finally be open and honest with me? Would he have powerful reasons for what he was doing? Like "what you don't know won't hurt you?" Or would he deny it all, and be so hurt we would be estranged forever. Would I have lost a father—a war casualty?

So I waited. I waited through growing lists of American casualties, lost battles, pictures of wounded and dying Allied men, stories of German atrocities that flooded the papers. I waited and tried to push the whole thing out of my mind. School activities, friends, Rudi—all these things seemed more real to me than what was going on at home and in the world.

And then, one morning I woke up to sunshine and shadows dancing up the wall of my bedroom and I could well believe there could be no war, no one could possibly have any problems. I breathed in the fragrance of the May morning and bounded out of bed just as the doorbell rang.

"Dietrich! Amelia!" I heard Father say, alarm in his voice.

"*Teufel's Drück!* The devil's dirt!" Onkel Dietrich's gruff voice boomed out as he stomped into the house.

Amelia's plaintive cry, "Oh, Tante!" came to me as I heard her rush into the house behind her angry father.

I ran down the stairs in my nightie without waiting to dress. It was Karl, I just knew. Something had happened to him. Oh, no, please God, no!

Amelia was crumpling some letters in her fist as she ran into Mama's arms sobbing.

"Look!" Onkel Dietrich bellowed, snatching the papers from Amelia's trembling hand. His face was red with rage and he was scowling as only he could scowl. "Look what they did to my Karl! Just look! War! *Gott verdammt!* God damn!"

Onkel grabbed the papers from Amelia, shoved them at Father, who slowly spread them open. Mama and I looked over his shoulder as he read aloud, "We regret to inform you, Corporal Grossbach has been wounded in the Battle of Chateau Thierry. He is recovering well in a Red Cross Hospital. We are enclosing a letter to you from him, and as soon as he is recovered enough, he will be returned home."

The second letter was longer and in Karl's handwriting.

> Dear Mother, Father, Amelia, Franz and Hubert,
>
> I am alive and safe! They had to amputate my leg just below the hip, because of the danger of gangrene spreading, but I am healing well (all that hard farm work! Ha! Ha!) and learning to walk on crutches. Please do not worry. I'll be home before you know it and able to do more farm work than you would believe. I am lucky (blessed, Onkel Chris would say) compared to many wounded men. Keep praying for the end of the war and I'll see you before you know it. Give my love to Aunt and Uncle Altenberg and Emma. Tell her the nurses here are pretty, but not as pretty as she is!
>
> Your loving son
> Karl

"We're trying to be grateful it isn't worse and that he is alive. But it's so hard," Amelia said, wiping her eyes.

Mama kept her plump arm around Amelia, guiding her into the kitchen, but I was too numb to move one step to follow them. Father guided Onkel Dietrich into his study for the privacy I imagined Onkel needed. Only Father could calm him down.

I stood as though paralyzed, my mind filled with images of my well-loved, long-striding brother Karl, legless, limping and lurching on crutches all the rest of his life, unable to go to college; unable ever to dance.

If I could just swear like Onkel Dietrich and get it out—my disbelief, my outrage. But all that came to me was a stab of fierce, hot anger, like a bayonet in my heart.

"I hate war," I shouted inside myself. "I hate grown-ups for making wars! I hate the Kaiser, tanks, guns, poison gas, and I especially hate—yes, I do—I hate Germany!"

The time had come. I had to find out just what my father was doing to aid and abet the enemy—this German enemy that took my brother Karl's leg! The German Methodist Church in America—the Methodist Church in Germany—was there a connection? I had to find out—for my own peace of mind. And when I did, I'd summon all my courage to confront my father, my very own father, no matter what. And if he denied, or reasoned with me—or confessed? I pushed the thoughts of what I would do firmly out of my mind and started for the kitchen to help comfort Amelia. I was determined to do what needed to be done to right the wrong done to my brother Karl, to Mr. Klemm and all those boys over there suffering and dying for the United States of America!

Fierce determination stayed with me all during the rest of the week at school, through Saturday baking and during church on Sunday. It stayed with me on Monday, Tuesday and even during my time with Rudi after Glee club on Wednesday. Rudi had heard about Karl and we grieved together. Still, I did not tell, even him, what I intended to do about Father. He just might appeal to my softness and talk me out of it.

Now, it was Wednesday evening, prayer meeting night and I was ready. I finally thought of a plan and had been working on it all week. I'd go into Father's study, his Holy of Holies, while he and Mama were at church and I would go through every scrap of paper I found there. I'd search carefully, every second, hoping, expecting, needing to find some proof—on paper—in black and white—whether or not my father was in some way aiding and abetting the enemy. I shut my mind to any thought about what I would do if I found out it was true. All that came to me was horrifying images of Karl Grossbach without a leg, Mr. Klemm dead in his grave in Arlington Cemetery, bayoneted babies, gassed and blinded men. I had to know the whole truth or I'd never rest.

I could lose no time. Two hours was all I had at most, an hour for prayer meeting, an hour for Kaffee Klatch after. Two hours to get it all found and read and returned for future reference.

Dust motes shifted silently up and down in a column as the early evening sun poured through the window above Father's desk. I remembered as a child climbing up on top of that mysterious place, clutching at the dust motes that looked to me like golden coins. Just to hold them in my hands would be like capturing a treasure from heaven. Then, the puzzlement, the dismay when I opened my hands and found them with nothing in them. I remembered it all. And I remembered Father's finding me there with open, empty hands, and taking me in his arms and carefully showing me each thing on his desk, the pens, the pencils, the little black notebook for writing his sermons, the holy books between brass bookends, the Bible in German, the German Methodist hymnal, the church discipline, the poetry of Heinrich Heine, the works of Goethe.

"These are very important to me," he said gently. "And they must not be disturbed. I need everything in order, so I can do my work.

These are the tools of my trade I need to help serve Jesus of Nazareth. Do you understand?"

I didn't understand, I was too young; but I got the meaning of the seriousness to him and it stayed with me all through the years. The Holy of Holies must not be disturbed. I almost, for a moment, lost my courage, tempted to leave this sacred place and forget my mission. My good and gentle Father could not possibly be a traitor. But then, the memory of his anger flashing out at me when I deceived him made me wonder if I knew my father at all. I told myself that I deserved it, and knew somehow that underneath the anger, there was hurt. But now—the notice in the store window came to me in a flash. Spies and Lies—fragments of information—aiding and abetting the enemy—tool of the Hun. I needed to know who my father really was and what he was doing behind our backs.

Time was passing. I'd left the door open so I could hear my parents return and leave this holy place quickly, if they came home early. I could hear Gramma Altenberg's clock ticking faithfully from the living room.

I trembled as I opened the drawers, one by one. Nothing there but the tools of Father's trade in the middle drawer, pencils sharpened to a fine point, pens, erasers, paper clips. Nothing in the drawer on the right side but stationery and bundles of three-holed, lined note book paper for his loose leaf note book, envelopes of various sizes. Searching that much took very little time.

The left side of his oak desk that seemed so enormous when I was a small child held his files; and there, buried somewhere, I would find my proof.

I didn't know exactly what I was looking for, but some instinct led me through the first half of the alphabet, through *A* for Altenberg, *B* for birth certificate (Emma's) down to the *L* for Letters. Behind the *L*'s, in the sub-files, I quickly spotted *G* for Germany. I was breathing fast. I pulled out the file, sat down in Father's swivel chair and started to read.

I couldn't believe my luck, or rather, my blessing, when the first letter I pulled out was in German, from Marbach, Germany, dated April 9, 1914.

> Dear Brother in Christ,
>   You say in your last letter, my dear Christian, that we in the Fatherland should resist the militarism of Kaiser Wilhelm, that this faction does not represent all of the people of Germany. I have taken your admonition to heart. But how are we to resist when our leaders say they will not tolerate a written constitution? Does it mean we must bear arms against our own government? Or must those of us who do not agree with our leadership leave the country of our birth as your own father did?
>   These are perilous times. I urge you, after this correspondence, not to write about politics, but to keep to things spiritual, to preach the Gospel and to "leave to Caesar those things which are Caesar's."
>   With Christian Love,
>
>   Rolf Heckstein, praediger
>   Methodiste Kirche, Marbach
>   Würtemburg, Deutschland

The next few letters were all marked, censored, and contained only news about village affairs. Then, after 1915, there were no more letters.

I returned the German file and went on to the next sub-file, *Recent*. Time was slipping away. My heart pounded, but I kept on shuffling through the letters with cold fingers.

And there, among the last few, I found it. The proof I had been looking for. It was a carbon copy of a letter to the Bishop of the German Methodist Church headquarters, Saint Paul, Minnesota. I read it carefully, the thin paper shaking. I read it twice, three times.

> Dear Brother Bishop,
>   In reference to our last meeting, March 12, 1918, I feel I owe it

to you, to my fellow pastors and to myself to carefully explain my position regarding the changing of the affiliation of our church from German Methodist to Methodist Episcopal. After careful thought and prayer, I realize I am, after all, a stubborn Dutchman. I clung to the old name and affiliation because I was proud of our German heritage and I didn't want to cave in to the blind, anti-German-American hysteria that has gripped our country.

Now, I can see, I may have been wrong. Too many people suspect we may have maintained a connection with the Methodist Church in Germany and have used that connection to serve the military, wittingly or unwittingly, and unless we change our name and affiliation, we cannot expect people to believe that it has *never* been true. As you and my fellow pastors well know, the German Methodist Church was established independently in the beginning and has remained so for these many years.

I am a loyal American. I love so much about this country from the beauty of the earth to the ideals of freedom of thought and speech and equal opportunity for education and prosperity for all.

But I must declare to you, and in writing, that my highest and most abiding loyalty is to a Higher Authority, the Prince of Peace, and in His name, I will continue to minister to the suffering and needs of my parishioners or any other suffering souls, whatever their national origins or political persuasion.

I need to state clearly, also, that I will do all I can to aid our country and the fighting men overseas in whatever non-violent ways available to me. I only pray I may have the courage to accept the consequences of choices I make in expressing my beliefs.

I pray my attitude and this correspondence will not further alienate any of my brother pastors who may not agree with me,

With respect and fellowship, I remain,

Christian G. Altenberg

I slipped the letter back into the file carefully, shut the file drawer, and walked out of the room, closing the door to Father's Holy of

Holies. I climbed the stairs to my room, my own sacred space. I didn't want to see my father when he came home from prayer meeting. I wasn't ready. I needed time to sort out the meaning of all that I had read.

"Highest of Loyalties," he'd written. He'd been torn apart by divided loyalties for months. I understood in a way I never had before. I'd been feeling that war inside me myself. I'd been torn apart, too, between loyalty to my father and his ideals, loyalty to America, my own birth home, and loyalty to Rudi, for whom I was feeling such a new, powerful kind of love, Catholic or no.

Father loved this country, his second "home." But he loved his religion, too. And how could he wipe out the warm memories and appreciations of his first fourteen years of life in another land? What was my highest of loyalties, I wondered. Could I stand up for what I believed with as much courage as my father had? Could I bravely suffer the consequences of choices I may have to make some day?

I thought I was losing my trust and respect for the father I had adored all my born days. Now, I began to see him in a whole, new light. How could I have doubted him, my own father? The chill, the distance that lay between us ever since the holy night at Rudi's church seemed like a chasm that could never be bridged. If he knew, if he found out, somehow, what I had believed about him, would he ever forgive me, ever trust me again? Would we be living in the same house aliens forever?

Aliens! The word had nothing to do now with citizenship or the law, but with a feeling, a feeling of being apart, not a part of.

I couldn't take my eyes off my father the next morning at breakfast. It was as if I had never really seen him before. The wrinkles in his forehead, the touch of silvery grey hair at his temples, the deep laugh lines around his eyes and mouth, the way his shoulders slumped when he was hurt or tired, the way he blew his nose after he'd laughed so hard he got tears in this eyes—all these made him seem like a real, down-to-earth human being. Was this the man I had once thought was God, and then thought might be a traitor to his country—or worse, even—a spy? Was this the man I had feared?

"More coffee?" Mama said, breaking the silence that often lay among us now that Amelia was not staying with us longer.

"*Nein*. No, Mama, I must go. So many more bonds to sell. I decided to sell the bonds, but not fill in the Blue Cards and accept the consequences."

He squared his shoulders, pushed himself away from the table and stood up. "I want to tell you, Mama, Emma. I've made another decision. Last night during prayer meeting, I made it. I'm going to fly the American flag in the sanctuary. On the right side. On the left I will fly the Christian flag, the white flag with the red cross in the center. That should satisfy everyone."

He smiled a weak smile. "Well, now. So much for that." He kissed Mama on the cheek, patted my shoulder and left the house.

I could see tears glisten in Mama's eyes after the door closed. Wordlessly, she picked up the cups and saucers and looked at me.

"I'll be at the armory, knitting this noon, Emma, but you'll be home after school?" There was just a hint of pleading in her voice. It hurt her to see Father hurt. For the first time in my life, Mama needed me, for something more than help around the house.

"I'll be home right after, Mama," I said as I kissed her soft cheek.

CHAPTER TWENTY-NINE

Allegiance

I MANAGED, SOMEHOW, to get through the day at school, but my thoughts kept going home. Heavy thoughts, heavy feelings, would they never end?

"What's the matter?" Victoria asked between classes. "You've had your glum look all day."

"Father's decided to fly the flag in church," I answered.

"Oh, my," Vicky said, "That's something. But why so glum about it? Seems like some kind of victory to me."

"Not to Father, Vicky. More like defeat to him. Mama feels it, too. Like caving in."

I didn't want to tell her about my search, my finding. Not yet. Not until I knew for myself when and if I would confess it all to Father. Rudi was away at the basketball tournament in Northfield, and I couldn't talk to him, either. I missed him.

I hurried home after school as I promised Mama. She had that wistful tone in her voice when I left her in the morning, so rare for her.

From the moment I walked in the door, I knew something was wrong. I heard a scuttling sound coming from the kitchen and Mama's indignant voice. Something terribly wrong was going on. It felt dangerous, somehow. Some instinct told me to stay behind the door, just to watch—and listen.

"Of course I'm not going to sign any pledge card just to prove I'm not hoarding flour!" Mama was saying, hands on her hips, angrier than I had ever seen her. "What right have you to—"

A heavy set, dark haired man was standing in front of Mama's kitchen cabinet starting to open the doors.

"Why, the very idea. How dare you! This is my house. My kitchen! Who gave you the right to bust in and rummage around in my cupboards."

Ignoring my mother entirely, the large man pushed aside boxes of baking powder and salt and soda and all Mama's neatly arranged spices, searching every shelf.

"Why the very idea!" Mama repeated. "I told you! I do not have more than a cupful of real flour in the house. Why are you doing this? Is this what you did to Mrs. Fritsche, scaring her to death—and her young son, too! What's the matter with you?"

The large, unknown man turned around and looked at Mama. "Nothing's the matter with me, Mrs. Altenberg. It's you—all you people in New Ulm—pro-German, anti-American trouble-makers. You're suspected of hoarding pounds of flour—sugar, too—you know—staples our boys overseas really need! I'm sent here to find out where you are storing them. Our country's at war, you know!"

"I know our country's at war! What do you think we are? Ignoramuses? I'm a minister's wife. My husband's a minister of the gospel!" Mama declared. No backing down for her.

"We've heard all about your husband, missus. Won't fly the flag— keeps preaching in German—in the German Methodist Church! We're keeping an eye on him, you can bet. Now, I'm still looking for hoarded flour. Where's your basement?"

Without waiting for Mama to answer, the man found the door to our cellar and started clumping down. "Why the very idea," Mama sputtered as I walked into the kitchen. She was still angry and close to tears.

"Why the very idea," Mama said again, then whispered to me as the man disappeared down the basement stairs. "Hurry over to church. Warn your father. Tell him to—tell him not to stay there. Who knows what big oaf will do next."

I flew out the back door, crossed the walk between the parsonage and the church and hurried in. Father was in the sanctuary. Two flags were draped across the front pew and Father was picking up the American flag, shaking it open.

"Don't, Father! Don't touch the flag! A man's in the house, turning it upside down. Go somewhere, he may come in here. Go anywhere."

That's all there was time for. Father looked at me, startled, letting one end of the flag slip from his hand in his astonishment.

My warning was too late. The front door to the sanctuary flew open and the lumbering frame of the strange man came striding down the aisle. He stopped in front of Father, looking down at the flag lying at Father's feet.

"See here, Reverend," he shouted, "what are you doing here?"

Father still held the corner of the flag with the stars in his hand.

"What are you doing to the American flag, Reverend. Don't you know it's never, ever supposed to touch the ground!"

"I'm sorry, sir, truly," Father answered, reaching down to lift the rest of the flag from the floor at his feet. "I was just looking at it. It needs cleaning." Never had I heard Father sound so humble.

"Who's supposed to believe that, mister. You refused to fly it in your so-called church," the man growled. "Now you're going to destroy it? Don't lie to me. You're a traitor!"

Indignation glittered in the man's eyes as he pointed to the American flag at Father's feet. "Pick up that flag, mister. Now! And I'll show you how to fold it. In case you don't know. It's a sacred symbol, Reverend. Of justice and liberty. It's in the pledge. Maybe you don't know the Pledge of Allegiance? Maybe all you know is German? Well, I'll teach you—now!"

He took one stride toward Father. I thought sure he was going to strike him—or worse—force him to his knees—force him to kiss the flag. Those ugly men had done that to Onkel Dietrich. My father was next!

I didn't think the man had noticed me—yet. I wasn't part of his outrage. I stopped breathing. Felt numb. I looked at Father—my own father—saw his shoulders slump, saw him reach down and pick up the flag that had slipped from his fingers and spread it carefully on the back of the front pew. I was paralyzed with fear. I felt trapped and helpless watching the horror unfolding in front of my eyes.

"Now place your right hand over your heart, mister, and repeat after me—in front of this young lady of yours," he said, motioning in my direction, but not looking at me. "I pledge allegiance—"

"I pledge allegiance—" Father repeated, his voice thin and weak.

"—to my flag—" the big man went on as though talking to a child.

Images swirled in my head—Onkel Dietrich on his knees—kiss the flag, *Gross-ass*—My skin crawled, but I couldn't move.

". . . to—to—my flag," Father whispered. And stopped. He squared his shoulders, cleared his throat and in his strong, deep bass voice went on, "I cannot do it! Not this way. Not under threat. It's not honest!"

The stranger exploded. "What do you mean, you cannot, it's not honest? You mean you can't honestly honor our country's flag? See here, Reverend, you're under suspicion for being a spy, in case you didn't know it—aiding and abetting our enemy—sending information to the church in Germany. And now, tearing down the flag of the United States of America! He dropped his voice and narrowed his eyes as he stared at Father. "You've got some explaining to do to the authorities. You'll have to come with me right now, I'm afraid. In case you disappear—get some other traitor to hide you. New Ulm's full of 'em."

"By what authority do you—" Father began.

But the man didn't let him finish. "This authority," he grumbled as he reached into his back pocket and pulled out a pair of handcuffs. "I've got the authority of the Commission for Public Safety of the State of Minnesota."

I watched the man reach for my father's wrist, swinging the handcuffs out of his back pocket—a jumble in my head—consequences—courage—Karl—Father . . .

I heard a voice—an explosion coming from deep inside me. "My father is not a traitor—he's absolutely not a spy. I know it! I can prove it! It's me—me, his very own daughter that's the spy. I've spied on my own father!"

Silence followed my outburst. My voice echoed in our little sanctuary. The man looked at me, mouth open. I felt Father's arm around my shoulder, like a shield.

"Emma," he said, calmly "Let's fold the flag. Let's pick it up carefully and have this gentleman help us fold it. You, sir, watch to see we do it right."

"Well, now—" the man said, ignoring Father. "Well, now," he repeated, slowly still starring at me. "Where did all that come from?"

I felt my throat tighten, tears wanting to come, but I swallowed hard and went on, "All this suspicion, that's where. Spies everywhere. It's a disease. And I caught it! Now leave us alone!"

"Well, now," the man said again, still ignoring Father, still fixing his eyes on me. "Let's see now. You say you have proof? What do you mean? What kind of proof? They'll be interested down at headquarters, you can bet."

"We need to fold the flag first, like Father said. Then, I'll tell you. You watch us, mister—sir. See we do it right."

Father took one end of the flag, and I took the other and we folded it carefully, slowly, while the man watched us, all his pumped up heaviness gone like air out of a balloon. When the ceremony ended, the flag folded and lying on the pew, Father motioned graciously for the man to sit.

"Emma, let's hear your story," he said. "This gentleman, I am sure, will want to know what proof you have. And I, as a matter of fact, would like to know also."

With fear and trembling, but relief as well, I sat down between the two men and the whole story poured out, from my own suspicions of my Father to the search through his private documents. Neither man interrupted me, but before I finished my revelation and confession, Father laid his arm gently around my shoulder again.

"The letters are Father's," I said, raising my head to look at the man, not yet wanting to meet Father's eyes "They're his to show you. I violated his privacy—search and seizure, that's what it was, but I know what's in it and I can assure you—he is no spy!"

It was the nameless man who broke the silence that followed my story. His voice was almost soft. "Well, now, I—I'll tell them down at headquarters. They'll decide what to do. But stick around. We'll be watching your house, you can bet."

He pulled his chin into his neck, stood up and glared at us, "You'll hear from us. Soon. We'll want to see those papers, for sure," he announced, looking at us both. "And you'll be watched, you can bet, so you don't run away. Or some traitor doesn't try to hide you. New Ulm's full of 'em." He turned and lumbered down the aisle, handcuffs dangling from his back pocket.

The sanctuary door closed with a thump. I turned around and into my father's arms, buried my face in his shoulders and sobbed, "Oh, Father, I love you so much."

"I love you, too, my daughter. And I'm proud of you."

CHAPTER THIRTY

The Last Lesson

I WALKED THROUGH the week in a daze. Peace was beginning to be restored inside me and between my father and me, too. We had a lot to talk about still, but at least I no longer felt like an alien in my own home. As Wednesday came nearer, though, my very last session with Rudi, relief about my father gave way to grief about the boy I now knew I was impossibly in love with. Today, I would have to tell him I could not go to Prom as his partner. I hadn't even asked Father. I couldn't risk upsetting him again, making him angry—or worse, hurt, and feeling apart again. But how could I say "no" to Rudi? How could I let him go?

I was nervous the entire lesson time. Rudi seemed to notice it, because he kept trying to be funny. I loved him for it, but it only made me feel more guilty.

Just before the end of our time together, Rudi sputtered, "Chust, chelly, choke," and burst out laughing. "Well", at least I've graduated from yelly and yoke for juh—juh—jelly and joke."

He snapped his book shut. My heart sank.

"You can't go to the prom with me, can you, Emma?'

"I guess not, Rudi. I'm sorry." I bowed my head. I couldn't face him. I might cry. Rudi was silent. I lifted my head and looked at him and saw the sad look on his face. Then the tears flowed. "Oh, Rudi, I want to—so much," I managed to say. "But you know, I can't dance. You dance so well and love it so much."

"That's not all, is it, Emma? It's that I'm Catholic. Your father would disapprove, wouldn't he? My mother has the same fear of my liking a Protestant so much, too. I don't always understand these grown-ups."

Silence. Then, "Well, this is it, then, Emma? I guess this summer we won't see much of each other?"

"I guess not, Rudi. I'm sorry."

"I'm sorry, too. I'm going to be awful busy playing around at lake resorts this summer and helping Mutti at home."

"I know, Rudi."

We stood at the piano, looking at each other. Not touching. He had not touched me one time since the night I met him at Holy Trinity. I longed for him to touch me now, but he stood there stiffly, not moving a muscle. I wanted to help him out of his discomfort, but I didn't know how. I would not let myself make the tiniest move toward him.

"Anything new about your brother?" I asked, to break the silence that lay between us again.

"Oh, *ja*, I meant to tell you. Father Lempke located him through the Red Cross and a French priest. He's somewhere in France as Larry Meyers. The priest there is trying to persuade him to write home. He is well."

"Thank goodness. That means that when the war is over and he comes home, you can go to the conservatory."

"*Ja*. Yes, I mean."

"We're proud of you, Rudi. Winning the scholarship and all."

"Thank you. Everyone has been kind. Someone sent some graduation money, anonymously. I think it was a Turner."

The Beckers, I knew. But I had promised not to tell.

"The people of this town are good people, Rudi. We know that. Most of them. Out state nobody knows that, it seems. It's hard not being understood."

Rudi nodded, said nothing, but made no move toward the door.

"Well, at least we've come together this year. We have more unity than ever before. Like my mother says, 'A common enemy makes good friends,'" I went on, trying with conversation, to hang on to Rudi.

"*Ja*. I guess so."

We both seemed to have run out of things to say. Rudi broke the awkward silence. "Well, this is it, then," he said again, smiled a small smile and turned toward the door. This was just as it had been a year ago and I thought, now, I was ready for it. I was a year older—wiser, stronger. This year was all we would ever have. Our worlds were too far apart. I couldn't hang on to him any longer. But how could I just stand there and let it happen? I was older, but was I really wiser—or stronger?

I was about to call out to Rudi, but just as he reached the door, he stopped, stood still a long moment, then turned back to me!

"I don't suppose there's any chance of your dancing with me just once, Emma, even if you can't go to Prom with me? You'd love it. It's like flying. The music does it for you. I could teach you so quick."

How had he guessed? How had he known that learning to dance with him holding me close, was the greatest longing of my life? Hope returned! My heart started warming and racing again.

"Oh, Rudi, I'd love it! But where? When?"

"Some evening, maybe. We could meet at the foot of Hermann's statue. There's soft grass. We could waltz all around, maybe. Just once. Before summer?"

It sounded so easy, so simple. So wonderful. Just this once. Just to be held in Rudi's arms one more time. Our last chance. In spite of everything, my past deceit, the hurt I caused my father, our estrangement, our reconciliation, I heard myself say, as if from a distant place, "Just once, Rudi? Of course. For sure. Some Wednesday evening."

"This Wednesday night, Emma? That's tonight? Can you? Will you?"

"Tonight? Oh, Rudi, so soon?" I started to panic. Where was the stronger, wiser Emma Altenberg? But the look on Rudi's face and that wise Emma was gone. So soon was best. I wouldn't have to think about it for a week. No time to change my mind.

"I will, Rudi, yes, I will." I heard myself say. "But can we make it late? It stays light so long now and I don't want anyone to—You understand?"

"You don't want anyone to see the Methodist minister's daughter dancing, alone, in the park with a Catholic boy. I understand. That's just the way it is. But you'll meet me. Tonight," he said, grinning at me and giving me a tiny salute before he went out the door.

When Mama and Father came home after prayer meeting, it was still only dusk. It seemed to take forever for them to tidy up as they always needed to do before they went to bed. As the moments ticked by, I pushed the thought of deceiving my father out of my mind. What worried me most was not being able to get away at all and leaving Rudi alone at the foot of Hermann before he gave up and went on home.

But the time finally came. I had gone to my room to finish my essay on "Why I Am Proud To Be An American" and it suddenly flowed, without effort:

I am proud to be an American because of the millions of people who have come here from everywhere on the face of the earth, looking for freedom of thought and speech and a better way of life than they had in the countries they left.

For my grandfather that better way of life meant that his children, both sons and daughters, could get an education. With education they could make wise choices and have a better opportunity to become what they want to become. Many others have come to the United States of America for the same reason and I am proud to feel that I am one with all of them, no matter what their background or where they came from.

There is a statue of Hermann the Great rising over the town where I live. In 9 A.D. Hermann, a courageous Cheruscan warrior, defeated the Roman legions against all odds. But he stands for more than war. He stands for freedom from tyranny and he stands for courage. Like Hermann, many Americans have had the courage to stand against tyranny, especially the tyranny of fear—fear that we can't make it, and fear of the forces around us that want us all to think and act alike. I am also proud to be German-American, and still be one with all of those others. We

first

are all hyphenated-Americans, and that's what makes us interesting and great. Like Hermann the Cheruscan in the tenth century,
I want to stand against the tyranny of fear and prejudice wherever
and whenever I find it.

There, Miss Armitage. That is the way I feel. And I don't care if I
win a prize or not!

When I finished my essay, I lay down on the bed with my clothes
on and waited. I listened to Gramma's clock strike ten. I got up and
opened the door slowly, listening for the small snores and sounds of
deep breathing that would let me know my parents were sleeping. I
crept down the stairs, opened the front door and escaped down the
steps.

I was out of breath after hurrying the long distance from our house
and up the steep hill to Hermann's Heights. The park was empty. I
lifted my skirts a little and tiptoed across the grass, moist with evening dew, to the gate surrounding the stairs to the statue.

Rudi was there, his guitar in his arms, the strap around his shoulder.

"Emma! You came!"

"I promised I would."

"*Ja*, yes, but—. Well, let's have our lesson," he said matter-of-factly,
reminding me that this was a lesson, and not a tryst. I hoped my disappointment didn't show in the darkness.

He strummed a soft chord or two and began playing a tune I knew,
Strauss's *Blue Danube Waltz*.

"Lead with your right foot, Emma, like this—right foot, left together,
left foot, right together—*one*, two, three, *one*, two, three—"

He held his guitar in his arms, playing as he danced around me.
And I, from a distance, looked at his feet, looked at my feet, feel-
ing more and more foolish, inadequate and dismayed by the moment.
The time was slipping by and I needed to get home and in bed in case
Mama or Father woke and found my bed empty.

Rudi watched my feet carefully as he danced until the waltz came to an end. Then, he lifted his guitar from the strap around his shoulder and put it carefully in its case.

"I can't dance with a guitar in my arms so well as with a beautiful girl I care much about. Here, Emma, it's much easier with a partner. Just trust me, and I will lead you. *One*, two, three, *one*, two, three." He held out his arms to me, and I walked into them.

"Let me call you sweetheart, I'm in love with you," he sang softly in my ear in his clear tenor voice. "Let me hear you whisper, that you love me, too—"

One, two, three, *one*, two, three. The closer that he held me, the easier the waltzing became, until I felt like shouting with joy. "Look at me! I'm dancing! I'm dancing! The Methodist minister's daughter is dancing!"

Sadly, the song ended. Rudi stopped singing. But he did not let me go. He took my hand and we walked together around the foot of Hermann's statue and looked down at our town lying below us. A few faint lights twinkled through the dark silhouettes of the cottonwood and elm trees that lined our streets. Not a single person seemed to be awake. But the night was so still, I imagined I could hear the whole town breathing, one breath.

"Look," Rudi said, still holding my hand, our fingers twined together. "Look at all the stars. If the stars could sing, wouldn't it be beautiful?"

Thousands, millions of stars spread out all across the sky, the Milky Way arching like a misty path right over our heads.

"It's so still, Rudi, so peaceful," I said, my voice a whisper. "You'd never know there was a war over there. How I wish it would soon be over and your brother would return—and all the others. And our Karl."

"We have a long way to go, Emma. Lots of battles. Lots of deaths. But we've come a long way. And if it hadn't been for the war and my needing to learn better English in such a hurry, I may never have gotten to know you, Emma. As a friend."

He turned to me then and took my other hand.

"As more than a friend, Emma?"

"As more than a friend, Rudi," I breathed.

He gathered me in his arms, leaned down to me and kissed me.

It was a long kiss, longer than the Christmas kiss, by far, even more transporting. I knew beyond a shadow of a doubt I could not stand eighty-three of these.

"I don't want to let you go, Emma. But I know I must. I'll walk home with you."

"Thank you for teaching me to dance, Rudi. I'll never, ever forget it. And you are kind to let me go."

"Kind, Emma?"

"Yes, Rudi. Kind." He never need know my mother's words had come back to me in that powerful moment.

We walked silently out of the park together, holding hands, watching stars. At the corner where we usually parted, we whispered good night to one another and Rudi started to walk away. I hoped and prayed with all my heart and soul, it would not be out of my life. My sorrow, my longing was too deep for tears. I had to do something. Now! This time, I could not wait for him.

"Rudi!" I called softly to him though the darkness. "I—I can't say good-bye. Please?"

He was at my side in one step. "Emma," he breathed and kissed me once, twice, on the cheek, lips, the tip of my ear. I lost my breath. I lost count. After a long moment he let me go and I looked up into his eyes that seemed to glow, even in the darkness.

"Turn around, Rudi. Look up at Hermann. Just a giant shadow this time of night. Remember last year at the picnic? I got sick and you helped me down? Could you watch me climb to the top by myself one day before summer? I need to do that for myself.

"*Ach*, Emma. *Gern!* Gladly. Soon." I heard the lilt in his voice as he answered. We walked out of the park together and went our separate ways, the lilt in his voice still sounding like chimes in my ears.

CHAPTER THIRTY-ONE

Finding Our Way

I CREPT INTO the house, up the stairs and into bed without waking my parents. I had gotten away with my secret meeting with Rudi. It was worth it, I thought. It was a night I would never forget, no matter what the future might bring. If Father found out, I'd accept the consequences, just as he said in his letter to the Bishop that he would do if he broke the law. That thought brought me peace in my heart and mind and I slept without dreaming.

It was when morning came and I passed my parents' bedroom that a flood of remorse chilled me to the bone. Father stood in front of the mirror above the dresser, practicing his th's.

"Will I ever get rid of my accent?" he asked his reflection in the mirror. He was trying so hard. "Ch—Cheezus Chr-r-rist!" He pronounced slowly, rolling his *r*. "No! Juh—juh—Jesus Christ! There. *Das ist richtig!* That is right."

I turned away from the door and started down the stairs with a heavy heart. My father—the man who set me on his shoulder and parted the branches of the fir trees to see a bird's nest and woke me in the early morning to watch the dawn come up. This was the man who held me on his lap and sang German lullabies to me, who—the list was endless. And this was the man I was betraying again.

"You look—well, you look all grown up this morning, Emma," he said with a smile when he joined Mama and me at breakfast moments later.

"You do," Mama added. "So grown up all of a sudden. Sweet sixteen. My, my," and she winked at me, pointing to her bosom without Father's seeing her.

A surge of love for both my parents washed warmly over me and

I knew, in that moment, just as I had in church with the flag, what I had to do. I couldn't wait for them to find out from someone, somewhere, what I had done behind their backs. The older, wiser Emma was with me now, again.

I swallowed the lump in my throat and began.

"Father. Mama. I need to tell you something. Now. Even if I'm late for school. I did another thing behind your backs. I did something you will not like, but I have to tell you, even if I disappoint you, or make you angry. I don't want to live in a house of silence, without trust."

Mama stood still, coffee pot in hand. Father put down his spoon and looked at me, the smile gone. I had started. I couldn't stop now.

"I'll tell you what I did. I sneaked out last night. I got out of bed after you were asleep and I went all the way up to Hermann's Heights in the dark to meet—to meet Rudi Meyerdorf—and he—he taught me to dance! That's what I did, behind your backs. Against your will! And Rudi asked me to go to the Prom with him, and I think I will tell him I will."

Both parents looked frozen like statues. My heart beat so hard and fast, I was sure they could hear it and see the throbbing in my throat. Wouldn't they ever say something? Would they be silent with me from now on until the end of my life?

I waited. They waited. The clock struck eight.

"I have to go, now," I finally said and started to pick up my books. I didn't dare look at them. My courage was all used up. But I was painfully aware of the deep silence in the kitchen where they sat as I left the house, the parsonage—my home.

I got through school, somehow, chattered with the girls, smiled warmly as I could at Rudi as we passed each other in the hall, and somehow got through the day.

It went on like this for the rest of the gray and rainy week. Father spent hours in the Holy of Holies. Mama worked silently in the kitchen. They were polite enough. They smiled, said "good-bye" when

I left for school, "hello" when I came home, talked about this and that at supper. But still, something was gone from the closeness again. And in spite of Rudi and the dancing, I ached to have it back.

The weekend arrived with no change in the weather. We needed the rain, but I longed for sunshine. Father would be busy pouring over Sunday's sermon, so I couldn't count on his setting a time to talk to me. His not saying anything about my deception, my sneaking out—dancing with a Catholic boy—made me feel like a prisoner in some strange way. Maybe Mama understood me, this time. She said nothing either, but maybe I could talk to her. We had become more like friends lately, but still, she was my mother—and Father's wife. Could I make her take my side against her beloved husband?

Friday night at supper, we talked about the weather, a little about the war, nothing about me. I started to get up to clear the table when Father touched my arm.

"Just a moment, Emma. Sit down. Sit down, Mama. I want you to hear this, too."

I sat down. Mama sat down. He cleared his throat and I knew this might be a very long conversation, a lecture, maybe putting his foot down in his fatherly way. Some punishment like I'd never had before.

"What you did was wrong, Emma. You know that. Knowing you, your guilty conscience is your punishment and that's enough of that. But ever since all this sorrow and fear has come to our town, I've had to do a lot of thinking. And re-thinking. Had many a sleepless night over it all, as Mama knows. I've thought about my own parents, your grandparents, leaving a village in Germany, friends and relatives that were dear to them, working hard, saving to get to this country so their children could get an education and find a better way of life here. They sacrificed much, endured much hardship to find their own way."

Gramma's clock struck six o'clock. I couldn't move. Mama hadn't stirred. Father went on.

"I've thought about all this much, but especially since the day with the flag. You were honest. You showed much strength—courage. Trust came back. Pride in my daughter. I want to tell you now—"

Tears were filling his eyes. He took off his glasses and blew his nose, his big nose. Then, he straightened his shoulders.

"I have tried to find my own way, too. Not anybody else's way. Often against the authority over me. But I've been stubborn, too—about Catholics—about dancing—about the German Methodist Church not changing its affiliation. I'm not young anymore, but I'm still learning. So, now I know, after all this thinking—and praying, Emma— you must find your own way, too. So—go to the dance. Go with the Meyerdorf boy. I will put on my frock coat. Mama will put on her best dress and we will join the other parents. We will walk into your gymnasium in front of everybody. We will sit in the front row of the bleachers and watch our daughter dance. No matter what some old-fashioned Methodists will think. *Ja*, Mama?"

Mama was beaming. Her whole round body seemed to glow.

"Those who find happiness today, need not wait until tomorrow," my mother said, in German.

"Proverbs are like butterflies, some fly away," Father answered, in English. He rose from the table, pulled me to him, gently pulled Mama to his other side and kissed us both on both cheeks.

I thought I could not hold the joy that filled me—and pride in both my parents. Father and Mama and me here together, now, and Rudi, soon. And in another tomorrow, the war and all its horrors would end, and the fear and silence would go with it. And Karl would come home, and in the years ahead, New Ulm would heal from these wounds.

Just as Father started toward his Holy of Holies, and Mama to her holy place, her kitchen, Father had one more thing to say, "Just remember the prayer. The Catholic prayer of Saint Francis, 'Lord, make us instruments of peace.'"

He looked at me, his eyes twinkling, and all my insides twinkled with him.

Epilogue

"Eighty-eight—eighty-nine—ninety!" Counting aloud to myself, I gripped the railing of the circular stairway I was climbing and looked up.

"Ten more steps to go!" I called down to Rudi, who watched and waited one-hundred feet below me. My voice sounded as though it came from inside a tunnel. The railing I clung to seemed to shake.

"Want me to come up, Emma? Stand behind you?"

"Thanks, Rudi, but no. This is something I must do by myself—alone."

I shut my eyes tightly against the fear that clutched at my stomach and took a deep breath. The chill that sped inside me like a spear of ice quieted a little. I forced my eyes open. The circling was over. Ten straight steps above me loomed the huge statue of Hermann the Great with his winged helmet and mighty spear raised defiantly above his head. I often worried that when people came to New Ulm and looked at that statue towering over our town, they would think that all German-Americans were militaristic war-lovers.

And, of course, since that day about a year ago, Hermann represented shame and defeat to me. I never liked heights. But now, close enough to really see his face, I saw something more there—not defiance and anger, but strength and confidence. Going the rest of the way was something I had to do. Looking at the steep but short distance I still had to climb, I spoke sternly to myself. "You will make it,

185

Emma Louise Altenberg. You must. It's been a long, painful year. If you can do this one more thing, you'll be ready for anything."

I grabbed a handful of skirt in one hand to free my feet, lifted my chin and resolutely took the last few steps. A black iron railing guarded the edge of the narrow walk just below Hermann's boots. It was something to keep me from falling. I looked far down at the ground below to catch a glimpse of Rudi's reassuring figure, waiting patiently, watching me intently. His feet were planted solidly on the ground. Sunlight glistened on the brass trumpet he held tightly under his arm. He waved, and his hand touched the feather in the brim of the hat he was wearing for band practice that day. The jaunty little feather seemed to wave, too. I couldn't bring myself to wave back, couldn't loosen my grip on the railing. The distant ground began to swim. I felt as though I would pitch forward—and down. From far away, through an empty tunnel of sound, I heard Rudi's voice, "Good for you, Emma. Now don't look down! Look up!"

I steadied myself, swallowed, took another deep breath and slowly, carefully inched around the narrow walk beneath Hermann's feet. I forced my gaze up from the ground that seemed to pull me like a magnet, and looked far out into the distance. My dizziness slowly ebbed.

Awe and wonder filled my whole being as I saw, for the first time in my life, all of my town and its surrounding countryside. Miles of the Minnesota River Valley lay below me. Far to the west stretched the great prairie, and at its edge was Sleepy Eye, the town named after an Indian chief. I remembered the countless stories I had heard of the Indian Massacre in 1862, the courage of the pioneers of New Ulm who thought they had been friends of the Indians. Did the Indians ever feel like we have felt this year, aliens in a land they loved—apart, not a part of?

I clearly saw the road that led from Sleepy Eye right in to town, becoming New Ulm's main street, the street of parades—the many, many parades I watched from Father's shoulders when I was a small child. Small sun glints from the river winked through the cotton-wood trees that lined it.

Beyond the river, on the other side of the valley, the woods began, bordering the edge of the Grossbach farm. How many times I had explored those woods with Father, and dear Karl, looking for morel mushrooms and wildflowers in the spring, hazel nuts, butternuts, black walnuts in the fall, calling whippoorwills at dusk and waiting for the oaks and maples to shout their glory when autumn came. Now, from this distance, in their late spring leafiness, the great trees looked like giant, soft cushions you could jump down into and land with a bounce.

This May morning, not a leaf in the woods stirred. Not one curl of smoke rose from a chimney in town. The spire of Holy Trinity—Rudi's church, rose above all the other buildings. The steeple of the German—soon to be just Methodist—Church, Father's church, barely poked above the trees.

The American flag hung limply from the top of the armory. You couldn't tell from this distance that the flag was red, white and blue, with thirteen stripes and forty-eight stars. I pushed out of my mind the ugly scene with Onkel Grossbach and the fear I'd felt for Father as we folded the flag in the sanctuary of our church. I wanted to remember the stars and stripes as a symbol of the best of America, my own birth home.

There was no hint in the tranquil scene I looked down upon of the heart-ache and turmoil, the fear and bewilderment my friends and family, all of New Ulm, and many, many German-Americans had endured in the long year that now lay behind us. Peace would surely come before this year ended.

I closed my eyes again, breathing in the fragrance of our town—the lush, damp woods smell, the comforting, grainy smell from the flour mill, the faintly sweet, malty smell of beer. The familiar odors brought tears to my eyes. The first tear drop rolled down my cheek and nestled in the corner of my mouth. I flicked out my tongue and caught it. It tasted of salt, like sauerkraut and pickled schnitzel beans.

The familiar taste and fragrances mingled together, quickening a vivid memory in my mind.

When I opened my eyes, the memory became an image, like a living painting. The vision was so real that Minnesota Street, which moments before had been silent and empty of all life, seemed to be filled with a parade of thousands of marching men. The air around me that had been dawn quiet a moment before now seemed to be filled with the sound of music, the music of that exciting but greatly misunderstood rally.

Tears flowed freely now, and as I stood there in the shadow of Hermann the Great, I made a promise to myself, a solemn promise: I, Emma Louise Altenberg, will tell this story some day. I don't know who will read it. My children? My grandchildren? But tell it, I must.

Promise made, I felt strength rise up inside me. I said *"Aufwieder-sehen"* to Hermann, waved to Rudi, and started down the winding stairway to meet whatever lay ahead.

An Historic Note

ALTHOUGH THE PRIMARY characters in this book have been fiction-alized, the events described are part of the historical record.

Few American cities claim a stronger ethnic heritage than New Ulm, Minnesota. Founded by Germans from Cincinnati and Chicago in the years before the Civil War, it maintained a sense of *Deutschtum*—

Germanness—in its cultural and social life. Symbolizing the city's prominent standing, the Sons of Hermann, a national frater-nal insurance society, erected a monument to the Teutonic hero, Hermann the Cheruscan, on the heights above the town in 1897. During the time of this story, the German language was spoken in homes, churches, and halls. Often, public events included addresses in both German and English.

Hermann Monument

New Ulm reflected the diverse cultures and dialects of the home-land. Members of the Turnverein, generally freethinkers, dominated the city's leadership. But, by World War I, nearly a third of the town had German-Bohemian roots with strong Catholic traditions. These families tended to be poorer and less educated, with many living in a neighborhood near the Minnesota River called *Gänseviertel*, or "Goosetown." In addition,

Lutherans, associated with the city's Wisconsin Synod college and church, constituted another major portion of the population.

When the war broke out in Europe, New Ulm's citizens generally supported Germany. In September 1914, community leaders held a rally at Turner Hall to raise funds for the German-Austrian Red Cross. The evening opened with the Second Regiment Band playing, "My Country 'Tis of Thee," followed by addresses from Reverend Adolph Ackermann, director of Dr. Martin Luther College, Reverend Robert Schlinkert, the local Catholic parish priest, and Reverend Christian G. Hohn, pastor of the city's German Methodist Church. Ackermann, in what a local paper editor called a "masterful" address, told the packed house that, "Germany did not start the war nor did the Kaiser want the great conflict." Reverend Hohn spoke on "The Need for Neutrality," but warned the audience "that serious results might occur in our peaceful United States" because of "colored and untrue reports published in America." A choir sang, *"Deutschland, Deutschland Uber Alles"* and *"Die Wacht am Rhein."*[1]

Rev. Adolph Ackermann

For more than two years, the United States maintained a position of neutrality. Indeed, President Wilson won re-election in November 1916 on the platform, "He kept us out of war." The tide turned swiftly, however, in the early months of 1917 when Germany altered its policy on the neutrality of American ships in the Atlantic, leading President Wilson to break diplomatic relations. The final blow came with the public release of a secret communication from the German Foreign Secretary to the Mexican government, proposing an alliance against the United States and dangling the return of New Mexico, Arizona, and Texas as a reward. Public opinion shifted heavily towards America's entry into the conflict.

As war clouds gathered, New Ulm's civic leaders held a public meeting and selected a peace committee to go to Washington to meet with Minnesota's congressmen. While the delegation was in the nation's capital, President Wilson called for a declaration of war, promptly approved by the Senate and the House. Within weeks, Congress passed a Selective Service Act, requiring men between the ages of eighteen and thirty to register for the draft by early June. Local draft boards began the process of actual selection, culminating in a call of 157 Brown County men in late July.[2]

Dr. Louis Fritsche

On July 25, 1917, community leaders held a rally on the grounds of Turner Hall, ostensibly to answer questions about the draft, but also to build support for a petition changing the law so that only volunteers would be sent to fight in Europe. Mayor Louis Fritsche, vice-president of the state's German-American Alliance, presided over the event, attended by nearly 8,000 people. Other speakers included Fritsche's brother-in-law, City Attorney Albert Pfaender, Albert Steinhauser, a newspaper editor and decorated veteran of the Spanish-American War, as well as Rev. Ackermann. Following Mayor

Fritsche's introduction, Pfaender gave a carefully worded address to the crowd, saying, "Nothing can be gained by resisting the draft. It is the duty of these young men to respond promptly when called."

Other speakers were less circumspect in their criticism. In an impassioned speech, Ackermann declared, "We do not want to fight for Wall Street, England, or France." F. H. Retzlaff, a prominent local merchant, told the audience,

> If all the money in the state of Minnesota were piled on this table and offered to me that I would be willing for my boy to go across the ocean and fight in the trenches, I would throw it in the face of the man who dared to tempt me.

Captain Steinhauser reminded listeners that the Declaration of Independence "gave the people the right to overthrow any government which did not work in the interests of the people, and institute a new form of government."[3]

The event ignited a firestorm throughout the state, as major newspapers quoted the strongest remarks out of the context of the rally and its frequent calls to patriotism. Speaking to a loyalty picnic, Daniel W. Lawler, a former mayor of Saint Paul, labeled the New Ulm rally as "a traitor's meeting . . . presided over by a traitor Mayor."

> They all talked about constitutional law but everybody knows that this is all rot, that they are disloyal to this country and that they are loyal to the German Kaiser. They are Kaiserites and not Americans.

The *Princeton Union* alluded to the destruction of the town during the Dakota Uprising in 1862, asking, "Is it any wonder that there are those who regret the Sioux did not do a better job at New Ulm fifty-five years ago?"[4]

In late August, Governor James Burnquist suspended Mayor Fritsche, City Attorney Pfaender, and County Auditor Louis Vogel

from office. Although the first two men submitted their resigna-
tions, hoping to deter further action, the Public Safety Commission
refused the offer, insisting on a formal hearing of the charges. In
December, the Governor removed Fritsche and Pfaender from their
positions, but dropped action against Vogel, who was not among the
rally's organizers or speakers. Under threats, the Board of Dr. Martin
Luther College requested the resignation of Rev. Ackermann. After
twenty years of service to the school, he stepped down and found
employment at a local bank.

While the United States mobilized for war, it also implemented
a campaign to quell opposition on the home front. Congress established the National Council of
Defense and authorized states
to create similar organizations
with sweeping enforcement
powers. The Minnesota Public
Safety Commission emerged as
among the most repressive in
the country. The suppression
of dissent created a climate of
fear, especially in towns with a
significant German-American
population.

Government agents moni-
tored newspapers and the
mails and took notes at events
such as the July rally in New
Ulm. Undercover agents—the

Albert Pfaender

state hired nearly six hundred during the war—spent hours in local
saloons and hotels, listening for any hint of disloyalty. The federal
government required all aliens over the age of fourteen to register
and threatened confiscation of their property. Some were interned.

The government also encouraged citizens to spy on the activities
of their neighbors. "If you smell bacon cooking in your neighbor's

A Perfectly Good American Citizen of German Descent Decided to Put a Concrete Floor in His Coal Shed.—By F. Fox

Saint Paul Dispatch, April 17, 1917

kitchen on porkless day, report him!" declared a newspaper column. "If you are invited out to a meal in your neighbor's house, and he serves you wheat on a wheatless day, report him!" When the county agricultural agent discovered that farmers Carl Beltz, John Lucas, and Frank Lucas had not planted some of their fields, he recommended an investigation into their loyalty. The mayor's son, Theodore Roosevelt Fritsche, remembered other dark episodes. "They thought there was a German spy behind every tree," he recalled. "Houses were painted yellow, a few of them around New Ulm . . . One man was even tarred and feathered because he was a German."[5]

The city was not united in opposition to the war. The Superintendent of Schools, H. C. Hess, served as Brown County Director of the Public Safety Commission, while civic leaders such as Willibald Eibner, Judge I. M. Olsen, and Fred Johnson organized loyalty meetings, inviting Governor Burnquist to speak to a large rally on the courthouse steps in New Ulm. Many businessmen complained that the town's reputation for disloyalty harmed local industry and commerce.

Further retribution against the city's deposed leaders came the following summer. When the county medical society refused to punish Doctor Fritsche, the state medical society withdrew its charter, leaving the licensing of every doctor in the county under a cloud. The Minnesota Bar Association brought Pfaender before a hearing, where he avoided disbarment by signing a lengthy apology and promising to give speeches to loyalty meetings. The sharply worded articles of Albert Steinhauser, editor of the *New Ulm Review* and the German-language *New Ulm Post*, brought expulsion from the Minnesota State Editorial Association in March 1918. When that reprimand failed to dampen his criticism of government policy, the editor was arrested

Before their departure for Camp Dodge on September 21, 1917,
Brown County soldiers paraded down Minnesota Street.

by federal agents, rushed to federal court in Saint Paul, and charged under the federal Espionage Act.

Once American troops entered combat—with New Ulm men in the ranks—the war came to a quick end. In the aftermath, the city's deposed leaders received some small measures of vindication. School Superintendent Hess paid a price for his role as director of the Brown County Public Safety Commission. In a school board election in 1919, insurgent candidates overwhelmingly defeated two pro-Hess incumbents and terminated his contract. Louis Fritsche ran for mayor in 1920 and won by two-to-one margin. In his first act, he appointed Albert Pfaender as city attorney. At a synod district meeting in 1920, Adolph Ackermann received a formal apology from his church. Steinhauser was never brought to trial, although several American Legion posts unsuccessfully demanded the termination of the old soldier's pension.

Christian Hohn

THE AUTHOR OF this book, Kathryn Adams Doty, was born in New Ulm in 1920. Her father, Christian Hohn, first served as the pastor of the city's German Methodist Church from 1901 to 1903, then returned from 1912 until 1926. A local newspaper editor described the minister as "a man of practical, everyday Christianity, a live wire." After World War I, the German Methodist Church disbanded and became affiliated with the Methodist Episcopal Church and moved away from German language services. The present church, at the corner of Broadway and Center Streets in New Ulm, was built during Christian Hohn's pastorate.[6]

Anna Hohn

Kathryn's mother was born in Friend, Nebraska, in a sod house. Her mother was a German-from-Russia immigrant and her father a man of the Jewish faith. Her contribution of boundless energy, hearty laugh and great interest in designing the kitchen of the New Ulm Methodist Church, made her a much loved minister's wife.

Notes

1 *Brown County Journal*, 19 September 1914; *New Ulm Review*, 16 September 1914.

2 *New Ulm Review*, 4, 11 April 1914.

3 *New Ulm Review*, 1 August 1917; *Brown County Journal*, 1 August 1917.

4 "Address of Daniel W. Lawler . . . at Loyalty Picnic, August 19, 1917," Public Safety Commission, Minnesota Historical Society; *Princeton Union*, 9 August 1917.

5 Dr. Ted Fritsche, Oral History Interview, 27 February 1993.

6 *New Ulm Review*, 20 November 1912.

PHOTOGRAPH CREDITS: Brown County Historical Society, pages 189-191, 193, 195